WELCOME TO THE SPLATTER CLUB II

EDITED BY:

K. TRAP JONES

ISBN: 978-1-940250-51-9

Artwork by K. Trap Jones
    www.theevilcookie.com

Interior Layout by Lori Michelle
    www.theauthorsalley.com

Printed in the United States of America

First Edition

Visit us on the web at:
www.bloodboundbooks.net

Also from K. Trap Jones:

The Sinner

The Harvester

The Big Bad

The Drunken Exorcist

OTTO WARMBIER

Sentenced—15 years
Teeth yanked out then jammed back in
Fly home. Hi Mom. Die.

—Ryan Dyer

TABLE OF CONTENTS

Meth Gator 1
Lucas Milliron

The Road Crossed the Chicken 16
Jay Wilburn

Igloo Made of Flesh 23
Zoltán Komor

War of the Wildflowers 25
Arlo Gorevin

A Pie-on the House 37
Patrick Winters

The People Around You 47
Lucy Leitner

The Sack Cutter 53
Nikki Noir & S.C. Mendes

Hell Comes to the Burger Hut 66
Matt Weber

The Long Winter Ahead 75
Thomas K.S. Wake

Genital Gorgonzola 90
Montague White

Jezebel 92
W.R. Macumber

Protein 100
Rachel Nussbaum

Lost Girl, Found Dog 117
Daniel J. Volpe

METH GATOR

LUCAS MILLIRON

1

IT WAS A good five minutes before Tommy noticed the blood leaking from his Fleshlight. He'd been pounding his meat so hard, he never felt the shards of glass digging under his foreskin, looking like a crunchy French tickler. His good eye bulged when he pulled out his pecker and beheld the bloodied member with bits of broken beer bottle sticking out his urethra. Tommy let lose a howl that rattled the trailers windows. Anna, his barrel-shaped wife with fried-egg titties and face like a toothless possum, burst into the room wearing her diner uniform.

"My dick!" he yelped, his voice hoarse from hitting the crack pipe.

Tommy flinched as he touched his bejazzled cock. Blood ran down his thighs, soaking into his crusty socks between his infected toes. Anna cackled with a gummy smile, pointing at her husband's dick. Tommy looked at her, saw the frog spear in her hand.

"You dumb fuck!" Anna laughed and stabbed Tommy's throat. "Didn't notice the pocket pussy sounded like a baby rattle? Told ya them drugs fuck you up!"

Tommy wiggled like a worm on a hook. Anna pushed against the spear, her bulk holding him in place with ease. His bloody hands clawed the air trying to grab her, his throat popping and whistling.

"Don't care what po'lice say," Anna sneered, "Florida law might think a husband can't rape his wife, but my black eye says otherwise. Ya' scrawny, pencil dick motha' fucker gow'na die!"

Anna pulled out a hammer from between her saggy tits and swatted his skull. His eye socked collapsed like a watermelon, shooting his eyeball out like a spit seed. Anna laughed, thinking of Gallagher with his mustache, overalls, and splattering mallet. She laughed and laughed, smashing his face into a mess of ground pulp.

But that wasn't enough. Spear imbedded through the recliner, Anna got on her knees and grabbed his nut sack, squeezing both testicles so they bulged out of her fist and rested against the chair's wooden frame. With one swing, the hammer splattered his balls like a popped tick. Anna cackled at the gooey mess between her fingers, beating his dick like a stubborn nail. Tommy's body was as limp as his cock, dead.

Anna huffed and threw the hammer on the floor. She tried to catch her breath, but there was still work to do. Her face and fingers felt sticky like she'd been playing in warm syrup. She cleaned up and changed into her favorite moomoo, then went to the kitchen where Tommy cooked his meth. Anna dawned his rubber gloves and aprons, grabbed a plastic trash bin and shop broom, then pushed all of Tommy's meth lab into the trash. Noxious fumes billowed from the can like a smokestack.

Anna held her breath, her eyes watering as she rushed outside for fresh air. She hacked and coughed, walking away a few feet before lighting a cigarette. Standing there in her pink flip-flops and flamingo moomoo, she smoked her cancer stick and waited for the meth fumes to die down.

The cold midnight air was bright with the beautiful chorus of trailer park trash. Husbands beat their wives, hookers serviced Johns, meth heads howled at the moon, and Mexican's danced the night away to mariachi and reggaeton. Anna finished her fresh pack of smokes before going back inside.

The entire house was caked with a greasy film. The kitchen counter bubbled and sizzled where noxious chemicals mixed. The smell of rotting eggs and bleach burned her sinuses, but she gritted through the miasma and carried the trashcan outside.

Anna was a beefy broad and had no trouble tossing all Tommy's crap in the back of his old beater, a 1990 F150 pickup truck. The metal bed hissed as the chemicals sloshed out of the trashcan. Anna couldn't find a lid, so she went back inside and cut her husband to pieces using a hacksaw from his toolbox outside. She sealed the parts in black plastic garbage bags, tossed them on top of the chemistry set, then made the long drive into the glades.

It was about two hours before Anna found a quiet place to dump her ex-husband. It was a run-off canal not far from the sugar farm. In the cover of darkness, she backed the truck up to the side of the embankment, dropped the tail gate, and tossed Tommy and his meth lab into the water. Long shadows swarmed the bags of meat. Jaws snapped in the darkness as massive gators made snacks of Tommy's dismembered body.

"Been a while since I cooked up a good meal." She cackled. "Eat up, little babies! Mama wants you fat and happy!"

Anna hopped back in the truck and drove off, skipping town before anyone was the wiser. Meth from Tommy's chemistry set mixed with the water. Gators swallowed gallons of it while they feasted on his corpse. Three sixteen-foot monsters felt their hearts race and eyes dilate, while the largest, a twenty-foot relic from the Jurassic era, devoured most of the meth water. Its muscles grew so large and dense, scales popped and flacked away.

The monster gator turned to its brethren and snapped at the closest one. It's powerful jaws bit into the other gator's skull, crushing it. In one motion, the monstrous Meth Gator ripped off the reptile's head. The other gators swam away, darting back toward the city. The Meth Gator devoured its meal, then the rest of Tommy's corpse. With the taste of man on its tongue, it sniffed the air, and swam toward civilization.

2

"How can we be in Florida and not call it a vacation?" Sister Eve asked Brother Michael at a red light.

"There's no time for vacation when you're doing the Lord's work," Brother Michael replied, rubbing sweat from his brow.

"I know." Sister Eve sighed. "But if we're doing the Lord's work, why can't we appreciate *his* work at the beach?"

Brother Michael pondered a moment. It was already 11 a.m., and the day was only getting warmer. The last few miles saw so much traffic, it was safer to walk their bicycles on the sidewalk than ride them.

"Gosh darn it." Brother Michael smiled. "You've gotta point!"

"We're going to the beach!" Sister Eve cheered.

Miami was a long way from Iowa and might as well be a different planet. Eve was lost in the colorful world of little Havana's art district, the smell of little Haiti's soup joumou, and the rainbow of men and women with strange colored hair and tattoos. Eve knew God painted with a fine brush, but never knew the Devil's temptations could look as sweet as cotton candy.

The heat in late August was stifling; the humidity down right depressing. With thoughts of sand between her toes, Eve didn't care. Sweat was a fair price for such a beautiful day. Michael was five years her elder, and cute in his own quirky way. Eve was especially fond of his smile, though it shamed her to think sinful like that. When the traffic slowed down, they both started riding their bikes again.

Eve watched Michael peddling in front of her. His white dress shirt was plastered to his back with sweat, hinting strong masculine features. She avoided it at first, but more than once she found herself staring at his rump; felt herself blush. Michael was a test, she was sure of it. Why else would God put her in the custody of such a good-looking man?

Half an hour later, they arrived at South Beach. The kaki-colored sand radiated with its own beautiful glow in the hot afternoon. Blue waves crashed in the distance. A wind seasoned with salt blew across their sun kissed faces.

Eve smiled, drinking in the beauty, but was distracted by the crowds of people in scanty bathing suits. It pained her to see more flesh than Sodom and Gomorrah; so many people were going to Hell. All she could do was show them Heaven's Gates and hope they walked in on their own accord.

They locked up their bikes and took off their shoes. The beach sand was blistering hot. Michael hissed as he hopped toward the water, Eve right behind. Shallow waves washed across their feet bringing cooling relief.

"This was a wonderful idea!" Michael smiled at Eve.

Eve smiled back, happy to have won his approval. Michael looked over her shoulder, distracted. Eve followed his glance to a crowed of people huddled around a camera crew. She'd never seen anyone film a movie before.

"Let's go see what all the commotion's about," Eve suggested.

"Sure." Michael shrugged.

Eve was ready to burst with joy. First the beach, now they get to watch real movie magic. Eve about skipped her way along the wet sand, more than once catching her hand before it reached for Michael's. Her heart was fluttering, and her palms felt sweaty, but it wasn't the heat. She took a deep breath, then let out a half scream when they came upon the congregation.

Three dark skinned men violated a milk white woman with bright neon green hair on her head, armpits, and lady parts. Her tattoos were downright vulgar. Two young women were crudely drawn performing lustful depravities upon one another butted right up against a Strawberry Shortcake cartoon character on her thigh. Little Strawberry Shortcake was her favorite as a little girl. The tattoo's placement so close to her intimate areas dirtied her memory of the show.

The male talents servicing her glistened like the pagan Gods of Rome. They worked like well-oiled machines exploring every orifice they could, regardless if their endowments fit. Eve had never seen the male sex organ in person. Her familiarity was limited to textbooks and poorly drawn graffiti. Seeing the other gender flaunted so passionlessly was downright revolting.

The woman's groans were a contradiction of pain and ecstasy. Worst of all was the benevolence! Crew members went about their day as if this was as normal as watching parents bake cookies. A second woman, not involved with the love making—though the sentiment was lost in the present act—drizzled the actresses sex with lubricant. While one of the male talents violated the woman's rectum, another man in a leopard print thong craned his camera over the actor's shoulder, so close they might have been snuggling.

The actress's moans were silenced as another male talent shoved his privates in her mouth. It wasn't until she sat up to service him that Eve noticed the third man underneath her, licking her body and grunting like a suckling piglet.

"We need to go." Michael grabbed Eve's arm.

Eve's head was spinning. A voyeuristic spell kept her eyes locked on the scene even as Michael dragged her away. Her eyes wondered to the crowd watching. This part of the beach was littered with naked bodies. It reminded her of a leather shop her father managed back home. Old people with sun broiled skin laid out with all their parts exposed. Women laid in rows, legs open, allowing their womanhood a drink of sunlight. Eve would never look at roasted chicken the same again.

"This was such a bad idea," Michael muttered.

Eve's heart sank. He was right. It was a bad idea. It was her idea.

3

Michael and Eve were used to staying at bargain hotels and motels. The Hot Flamingo wasn't any different. It was two bright pink two-story buildings opposite one another with a small office trailer done up like a tiki hut at one end. It was decorated with fake wooden columns and cheap, broken tiki torches. It was tacky, yet Eve found it somehow charming.

The afternoon sun was hidden behind storm clouds so dark, it had Eve checking her watch to see what time it really was. Worse, promise of rain brought with it even more humidity. Both Eve and Michael were dripping sweat by the time they made it to their rooms. Their bike ride was long and quiet, and Eve still felt violated by voyeuristic urges.

"I need a soda pop," Michael said, wiping his forehead with his sleeve.

A soda? Eve thought. *He never eats sugar. I got him so twitter patted. It was all my fault! Why did I have such a bad idea?*

"I'm sorry about this afternoon." Eve glanced at her shoes in the doorway to her room.

"Tomorrow's a new day." Michael unlocked his room next to hers. "I think we just need to clean up and start fresh tomorrow."

"I still have some bread and deli meat," Eve offered. "I can make us sandwiches if you're hungry?"

"No thank you." Michael half smiled. "I don't have much of an appetite."

"Okay." Eve frowned.

"Looks like a dozy of a storm coming." Michael glanced at the clouds. "We'd better hunker down for the night. Not sure we're gonna make any more rounds this late in the afternoon anyway."

"Alright," Eve sighed. "Enjoy your shower."

"Good night."

Michael closed the door. Standing in the empty walkway overlooking an even emptier parking lot, Eve never felt so alone. She pulled out her room key and walked her bike inside. The room was simple; brown carpets, bamboo paneling, and a single queen-sized bed. There was a TV, minifridge, and a salmon-colored bathroom with more flamingo flourishes.

Eve sat on her bed, still thinking about the afternoon. She knew about pornography, but never dared watch it. The internet was full of such taboos, so she did well enough to keep herself offline; no social media, not even an email account. Her phone was a basic brick that could only text and make calls.

The woman's face played in her mind. Her body—so firm and augmented by plastic surgery— was a vessel of lust. Those men she knotted herself with, they, too, were burned in her mind. It was like watching the woman's body swallowing bottles of shampoo in every orifice. And their muscles glistening with sweat looked like glossy chocolate and caramel.

Eve's mind wondered to the bike ride. She remembered the shape of Michael's rump. The way his sweaty shirt stuck to him like a second skin. Eve laid on the bed, her heart raced after her imagination. Her skin felt clammy remembering when he grabbed her arm.

What if he kissed me instead?

Eve's fingers felt the smoothness of the sheets. They were stiff and free of wrinkles, just like Michael's shirts before prayer. Her hands felt the meat of her thighs. Her skin was soft. If Michael tried, he could bruise her easy.

What would that feel like?

She squeezed her thigh. It felt good. Her nails raked across her skin, tracing thin red lines.

She remembered the woman's face and cries as the men worked their way in and out of her body. Eve lost control of her own imagination.

Michael stepped into her room. Eve rushed over. He grabbed her by the waist, his strong hands pulling her close. She pressed her lips into his, breathed his air, tasting his spearmint mouthwash. They walked over toward the bed; their bodies tangled in lust.

Eve slid out of her panties, cupping her hairy lips with her hands. She blushed. No man, save the Lord Himself, ever saw her vulnerable parts. Michael unbuttoned his shirt, exposing muscular flesh. His nipples were like Hershey's kisses melting under her lips. As Michael worked his buckle—a woman yelled outside the motel room.

Eve shot up in bed. She was alone and her hands felt slimy. She looked at the bed. It was damp where she was lying.

Did I spill something?

It wasn't until she looked down at her legs that she noticed her panties hanging off her left ankle.

"Oh no!" she gasped.

Eve slipped her panties on, knelt over her bed, and began to pray.

"Have mercy on me, O God," Eve muttered, her hands clasped and eyes shut. "Accor—"

She stopped mid-sentence as the woman outside yelled again, louder than before. Eve rushed to the window and peaked out the curtains. It was the film crew from the beach! Eve didn't recognize them at first, not with their clothes on. The woman was in a blue tube top and neon yellow miniskirt, while two of the male talents wore blue jeans and baggy tank tops. The men from the beach pushed her against a hot pink Cadillac.

"I told you already!" she yelled, "I don't have your money!"

"We'll just have to take payment via, installment," said the taller man.

Eve rushed out the door.

"Leave her alone!" she yelled, shaking her fist in their direction.

"Cut!" A skinny man in neon green cut-off shorts shouted behind her—the one who'd worn the leopard thong.

Feeling eyes like bug bites, Eve froze and looked around. She'd stumbled right in the middle of another film session. There were two camera men and a boom operator just out of view of her window. The scrawny man, the director she assumed, threw off his red headphones and slammed his clipboard on the ground with a heavy stomp. He ran his hands through his greasy hair. Purple and red boils littered his pitted face like someone tried to put out a fire with a pitchfork.

"Hey lady," he said, approaching Eve. "What are ya doing? Can't ya see we're filming here?"

"Knock it off Zachary!" shouted the actress. "She didn't know. Besides, we got some fucked up weather coming. Lighting's gonna be off and we can't get the gear wet. Let's wrap and pick it up tomorrow."

"Your money sweet cakes." Zachary sucked his teeth.

The woman walked with purpose on eleven-inch heals, graceful as a panther. She slapped his face, grabbed his genitals, and twisted clockwise. Eve thought his eyes might have popped out of his face.

"Don't ever call me that again," she said as if reciting a recipe for muffins. "I, am the mother fucking director, producer, and queen bitch up in this. You disrespect me, this job ain't the only thing you're loosing. Got it? What's my name?"

"Yes," Zachary squeaked.

"What's my name?" She twisted more.

"Yes, Cinna-Bun."

Cinna-Bun released him, and Zachary collapsed on the floor. The other cast and crew cringed, covering their own crotches.

"I-I'm so sorry," Eve stuttered. "I-I had no idea!"

"No sweat, sugar!" Cinna-Bun smiled. "You've got guts. Small thing like you standing up to two big ass dudes for a total stranger? I'm flattered."

Cinna-Bun offered a handshake.

"Thank you," Eve sighed and shook her hand.

"And your name is . . . " Cinna-Bun cocked an eyebrow. "Sister Eve?"

Eve looked at her blouse. She forgot she was still wearing her name tag.

"Even braver for a Jehovah's Witness." Cinna-Bun snickered.

"Just reacting." Eve blushed. "I don't like people being taken advantage of."

"Oh, bless your heart." Cinna-Bun shook her head. "Hun, I'm gonna stop ya there before this get's all baby Jesus gibber gabber."

Lightning flashed, followed by a roaring crack of thunder. The sky was about to unload.

"Get this shit inside!" Cinna-Bun snapped her fingers. "Maybe we won't get all that thunder in the room."

Cinna-Bun assisted the crew. As Eve went back to her room, she thought more about everything she ever assumed about adult entertainers. Nothing. She never considered the kind of personality it took to work in such a life of lust. Then her tummy grumbled, and all she could think about was sandwiches. Another crack of thunder, closer and louder than before, setting off car alarms and rattling her windows. Eve rushed to her room, made her sandwich, without crust, and ate in bed, listening to the sounds of rain.

4

A few miles up the road, the bolt of lightning exploded the base of an old dead pine tree. It fell into a retention canal. Trash piled up behind the tree, forcing the blockage deeper into the drainage system that carried floodwater out to sea. The storm was relentless, but the Meth Gator was undeterred.

The massive gator followed the stream spilling out of the canal and into the city streets. Debris as large as minivans were washed away by the heavy current. Meth Gator swam with ease, its nose sniffing the air for flesh.

Before long, the parking lot of the Hot Flamingo flooded. The water continued to rise, slapping against the first-floor windows. Eve heard the water rushing under the door like a bath. She hopped out of bed, the water already up to her ankles.

Eve went to the window and drew back the curtains. It looked more swamp than civilization with water inches below her window. She couldn't open the door; she'd only get knocked down the rush of water. Eve tested the window. It was screwed shut.

"Darn it!"

The water was almost at her calves and still rising. Eve looked around, grabbed the office chair, and threw it out the window, shattering the glass. She threw bedsheets over the broken glass to protect herself as she jumped through into the storm.

The current pushed her back against the wall. Eve grabbed the door handle and pulled herself to her feet. She watched as her neighbor, Zachary the director, opened his door. The torrent of water knocked him on his ass. There was something else in the water. It looked like a log, until Eve saw the tail swish through the water.

A twelve- foot alligator rushed for the open door. Eve watched as Zachary scrambled to his feet only to be taken down by the reptile. He screamed, but his voice was cut short as the gator's jaws clapped around his face. The reptile spun its death-roll, ripping off Zachary's head and a two foot length of spinal column. The window exploded, followed by two of the actors and a camera man. Two more gators surfaced from the parking lot, growling in baritone as they snatched the actors by the legs and pulled them under.

"This way!" Eve shouted at the camera man, pointing towards the stairwell.

He rushed fast as his muscular calves could carry him, slowed by the current like running through a nightmare. Eve reached, and as she grabbed his hand, Meth Gator exploded from the water. It snapped its jaws, bit the man's torso, and death-rolled. In one quick motion, his grip was yanked from Eve. The man spun like laundry, water burning his nose and lungs while his face scraped against the concrete floor.

Meth Gator continued to roll, sending a wave of water that pushed Eve toward the stairs. She screamed as she watched the camera man's battered face emerge from the water. Another gator surfaced. It bit the man's arm and rolled. He screamed as his arm was ripped from its socket like a bottle cap. Blood gushed from the wound and disappeared in the black floodwater.

Something grabbed Eve's shoulder. She flinched, then turned and saw Cinna-Bun.

"Move your ass, bitch!" Cinna-Bun ordered.

They rushed toward the stairs, listening as the camera man's bones snapped and crunched, his scream muffled by blood and water. The girls grabbed the handrail and hoisted themselves out of the water and up to the second floor. Meth Gator dropped the carcass and turned in their direction. The water was rising, and the prey was escaping.

Meth Gator lunged for them. They were halfway up the steps when the gator's shoulders collided with the handrails, stopping it inches from their heels. It thrashed its head, bending the metal rail to its breaking point. The girls didn't look back, they kept running even as they heard the metal snap and the reptile's baritone hiss chased after them.

"In here!" Cinna-Bun shouted as they reached her room.

Meth Gator snapped its jaws before Eve slammed the door in its face. Meth Gator pounded against it with its massive maul. Eve drew the chain lock and stepped back, muttering prayers that the door would hold.

"I think we'll be ok." Cinna-Bun put her hand on Eve's shoulder. "Stayed here once before. Cops tried to bust the door but couldn't get in."

"Where's Michael?" Eve asked.

"Who?"

"My friend."

"If he's still downstairs," Cinna-Bun sighed. "I don't think he made it."

Eve's eyes brimmed with tears. Cinna-Bun frowned.

Meth Gator continued to pound the door. The frame began to splinter.

"Did you see the size of that thing?" Cinna-Bun grabbed Eve's hands and looked into her eyes. "I've only ever seen that look on crackheads. Alright, calm down. Door won't hold out long. We have to keep it together"

Eve nodded.

"You have anything we can defend ourselves with?" she asked

"Got a shit ton of dildos." Cinna-Bun shrugged.

"What?" Eve put her hands on her hips and looked Cinna-Bun side-eyed.

"You've not seen my toys!" Cinna-Bun chuckled

She opened a tall metal trunk on wheels. Round LED's illuminated the inside like a Hollywood makeup booth. Sex toys in every shape, color, and material imaginable glinted in the light. Rubber penises were Cinna-Bun's specialty. Some were hyper realistic down to the veiny glands and porous skin, while other monstrosities were the girth of Eve's forearm.

"What in heaven's name is that!" Eve's eyes bulged as Cinna-Bun brandished a three-foot rubber dick.

"Moby!" Cinna-Bun grinned.

"You don't actually use that." Eve blinked rapidly.

"Well..." Cinna-Bun smiled. "It is more of a prop than a toy...but I've taken a little more than just the tip."

Eve burped and covered her mouth, trying not to lose her lunch.

The pounding stopped. The girls looked at the door, then each other. Eve tiptoed toward the window and drew back the curtain just enough to peak outside. Another gator was climbing up the stairs. Meth Gator slapped its tail against the rail as it turned itself around, breaking it from the concrete landing and over the edge. Eve could see it splash just inches from the second floor. The water was rising faster than they expected.

Meth Gator charged the other gator. The smaller reptile hissed and puffed out its body to appear larger, but Meth Gator snapped its jaws over its head. It thrashed for a second before Meth Gator snapped its neck, killing it instantly. The girls gasped at the sight.

Meth Gator looked up through the glass, then flung the carcass into the window. The girls narrowly missed the explosion of glass. The dead alligator's body convulsed like a fish out of water. Eve screamed as Cinna-Bun swung Moby, smacking the dead gator's tail out of her direction.

Meth Gator rumbled its deep, guttural voice. They screamed as the gator climbed the wall and squeezed through the window. Cinna-Bun dropped her rubber dick and ran toward the bathroom.

"Come on!" she shouted to Eve.

Eve turned to run but tripped over the massive cock. She rolled over and watched as Meth Gator trotted toward her. Eve grabbed the dildo. As the gator opened its massive jaws, she tossed it into its mouth; David hurling a stone at Goliath. The dick soared through the air like a javelin right into Meth Gator's throat.

Meth Gator coughed as it tried to breathe. The floppy ball sack was caught against its teeth. Eve watched as the gator's eyes bulged, gasping for air. It thrashed its body, hurling the bed into the walls and smashing its tail against the TV.

Eve watched Meth Gator throw itself this way and that, slamming its maul into the ceiling trying to dislodge the robber cock.

Cinna-Bun reached for Eve and dragged her back toward the bathroom before Meth Gator could throw itself on top of her. It clawed the ground, its body weakening by the second. Its throat burped and sucked until it collapsed, choking to death on Moby Dick.

5

The rain stopped hours ago, but the girls couldn't stop looking at the massive gator to be sure it was dead. The first signs of morning crept through the broken window. Water crawled its way up to the second floor, covering the floor in a thin sheet of water. Eve and Cinna-Bun walked around the gator and went outside.

The Everglades took back The Hot Flamingo. Cinna-Bun grabbed Eve's hand and rested her head on her shoulder.

"I always answer the door naked when you guys knock," Cinna-Bun confessed.

"We get that a lot." Eve smiled. "Worst vacation ever."

The silence was interrupted by the sound of engines in the distance. Eve and Cinna-Bun looked in that direction. It was an air boat with three people on board driving straight for them. As they approached, Eve saw Michael onboard. She smiled, covering her face as she began to laugh, then to cry. Cinna-Bun pulled her into her chest and kissed the side of her head. Eve unleashed a torrent of tears, happy Michael was alive.

The air boat pulled up next to them. Two rednecks in forest camo and bright orange rainboots helped Michael get the girls on board and gave them headphones with built in walkie-talkies. The airboat skidded across the water over the other alligators, and on toward civilization.

"I stepped out to get a soda pop from the vending machine," Michael explained. "I had to go to the other building, but the flash flood dragged me a mile upstream. These guys saved my life."

"Newsman said Hurricane Mary wasn't supposed to hit for another two days," said one of the rednecks, sipping a can of beer. "Weatherman don't knows shit from peanut brittle."

Eve listened without hearing, looking at Michael. He met her stare, his soft honey color eyes glinting in the morning light. It was a miracle any of them survived. Before he could protest, Eve leaned in and kissed him on the lips. Cinna-Bun cheered. Michael gasped, but succumbed to the pleasures of flesh, just the way God intended.

THE ROAD CROSSED THE CHICKEN

JAY WILBURN

TEN-YEAR-OLD AMOS had a dog he named *Chicken* after resurrecting the animal. Amos also loved the eleven-year-old girl named Emme who lived across Red Stretch Road from his family's double-wide. This is everything you need to know to understand what went wrong last Thursday on the *Stretch*.

The dog used to be named Saban back when he had four legs, but that was before the Silverado crushed its skull and took its two front legs on the westbound lane of Red Stretch. After that, he wasn't the same, so Amos changed his name.

Amos Canter's and Emme Alabaster's families had the only two homes between the church cemetery and the black folks' liquor store. East past the church, there were a few scattered trailers, houses, and proper farms before you got to real neighborhoods in Leighton. The first of those were a good ways away. Going west, the black folks' trailers followed the liquor store. There were a few Sun Station convenience stores near State Road One-Eleven C, but then you had to get to the Food Lion out in Red Bluff before you were anywhere most drivers taking the Stretch were willing to stop. That was a farther ways.

That's why the Silverado didn't stop after killing Saban and why no one except Amos could hear or see Emme screaming as her daddy beat her in the dirt drive that led to their detached garage. Maybe Chicken could hear it too as he tottered on his two hind legs beside Amos, but that was hard to tell. The dog's eyes were missing, and its head was caved in like a soup bowl. That made his grimy snout look like a beak. Its one remaining ear twitched, but that didn't mean nothing. Chicken's ear did that even when there wasn't anything to hear.

Amos heard it and he saw. He didn't like it, but he didn't cry either. His momma and daddy didn't pay much mind to his crying or yelling or even laughing much. He was a boy. He wasn't supposed to cry. Meant he was tough. His folks didn't want a bunch of laughing or talking in their house. Wasn't enough room in the trailer for all that. Folks at school thought there was something wrong with Amos—something special wrong.

An officer visited about it. Amos's daddy told the boy to keep his ass out of sight and that devil dog, too. The officer knew his daddy from high school. They shared a beer and the officer left. Amos stopped riding the bus to school after because he was going to do his learning at home. That mostly meant keeping the chickens, helping with scraping cars, and staying out of the way.

Emme was crying hard that last Thursday. She bawled until her face was red, but her daddy kept swatting her.

As the swatting continued, Chicken stumbled toward the shoulder of the Stretch. Amos put a hand to the animal's hairless belly and guided him back. Chicken hissed and clicked in the back of his throat twice as a Grenada raced by from Red Bluff toward Leighton. They had two junked Grenadas in the scrapyard behind the trailer and the animal pens. One was burgundy and the other black where it hadn't rusted.

Emme had a proper house made of wood on a stone foundation. It had a real porch too. The wood had been stripped down raw, but never repainted, so it split from the weather and had patches of color in a hundred different shades of brown, tan, and grey. A Confederate Rebel flag pointed a skyward angle from the holder on one of the porch posts.

Emme's daddy dropped her in the dirt. He either stopped hitting her or paused from it. Amos couldn't tell which yet. Mr. Alabaster resumed yelling at her until he was red in the face. She turned her wet face down into the dirt and hid herself in her brown-blond hair.

Amos wondered if her tears would make mud the way Jesus did with his spit before he healed blindness and leprosy and whatnot.

THE ROAD CROSSED THE CHICKEN

A Datsun zoomed by from Leighton to Red Bluff maybe a foot from Amos's face. It musted-up his hair and the rebel flag across the street even gave a small wave. Chicken hopped backward a couple times trying to keep his balance. He gave a rolling whine and a snap.

They didn't make Datsuns anymore, Amos thought.

One of the white chickens ran past Amos's feet and sprinted out across the faded grey asphalt of the Stretch. He knew what was going to happen before it did. In situations like this, he just knew.

A Brookwood with its oddly squared lines drifted out over the middle line to get away from Amos standing so close to the road. The driver honked as he went by, creating an abrupt and exaggerated doppler. Going wide on Amos caused the yardbird to catch the inside of the tire. Feathers swirled out from under the car as the bird bounced three times between metal and road before tumbling out in the wake. The car raced on without stopping, but the bird came to rest on its back on the center line.

Its belly burst open and modest curls of intestines wrapped around the exposed liver. Above and around that mess, were the pale folds of the crop squeezing out of the rupture and the still lump of its heart.

As the flag on Emme's house gave another twitch from the road wind, feathers snowed down on both sides of Red Stretch.

Emme's daddy looked up because of the Brookwood's horn and his eyes lighted on Amos on the opposing shoulder of the Stretch.

Chicken, the two-legged dog, lapped out his meaty tentacle of a forked tongue. The tongue slithered around wild like it was tasting the air. He skipped toward the dead bird, but Amos put out a blocking forearm. Chicken groaned and hacked twice. The serpentine tips of his tongue lapped under Amos's earlobe before the boy finally gave the animal a proper shove. The two-legged dog staggered and danced on his legs a few feet from the road, overcompensating a couple times, but never falling. Chicken hissed and snapped.

Emme's daddy shouted, "Mind your own, boy. Get that chupacabra-looking-piece-of-shit out of my sight. Nothing going on here is any of your own."

Amos ignored the man and focused on the bird. Emme's daddy wasn't done. Amos knew it. In situations like this, he just knew.

Amos whispered, "Come on now. What you doin' sleepin' so?"

The bird twitched, but it could have been the wind. The rebel flag didn't move none.

"What now?" Amos said a little louder. His eyes watered as he squinted against a pounding headache that was just part of it. "You gonna come when you're called now, hear?"

The lips of the gaping wound slid back like the guts were going to squeeze all to the outside, wet and glistening. The lump of heart gave a couple spastic throbs, but then didn't do much more.

"Do what you gonna do, old hoss. Get at it!" he shouted as the world blurred out in his tears. His daddy would be surprised to see Amos was capable of tears. If he peeked out the window now, he'd think the boy was crying about the dead chicken. He'd be furious about the chicken and the tears.

Emme's daddy's jaw dropped open when he heard what the Canter boy said. Part was shock at hearing the kid could form words at all. The rest was being challenged by this half-wit midget he wished would stop eye-balling his daughter. "The fuck you say to me, boy?"

Emme lifted her dirty face from the dooryard. "He's just talking to the chicken like he do."

"Mind your own, girl, before you get some more. That mutant dog needs to go, too."

"Alright, I'm only asking once, so you better listen up." Amos's voice drew thready and old in his own throat. "Come forth!"

The bird gave a strangled caw and scrambled about where it lay, casting off more feathers. Its guts stuck to the street a moment, but then peeled away with a ripping noise once it found its feet. It wavered in an uneven circle in the middle of the road looking like she was heading to the Alabaster's property a moment. Then, it wobbled toward home.

"Jesus H. Christ," Emme's daddy breathed.

The chicken faltered, moved, faltered, and moved again, not quite clearing the street.

The bird paused and pecked at its own beating heart in the bundle of guts swinging between its legs and gave a surprised screech that sounded more like an owl or a raptor than a chicken.

A Durango approached the scene from over toward Leighton in

a rising roar of engine noise. The chicken tilted its head one way and then the other, not trusting the motion of its exposed heart.

"It'll be worse if you make me do it a second time," Amos said.

The bird hobbled to the grass as the vehicle ripped by in a blur. Another shrill sound followed another ill-advised peck at its own heart.

"Your name is Dawg now. Get on around back, Dawg."

Dawg the chicken hobbled, wavered, and hobbled some more.

Chicken hissed and Dawg gave a rattling growl that ended in a sort of burp. Amos giggled and Chicken backed up a couple steps giving the bird a clear path to wherever it wanted to go.

"Go inside, retard," Mr. Alabaster barked.

Amos turned his attention across the Stretch at Emme's daddy toed-up to the edge of his side up the road. The boy just stared with his mouth in a relaxed straight line.

In the silence of their locked eyes, a Cosmopolitan raced toward Red Bluff and a DeSoto swept by a couple seconds later toward Leighton, engulfing the two of them in a swirling cloud of exhaust.

"Leave him alone, Daddy. He didn't do nothing."

"Shut your mouth. You don't tell me; I tell you. And I'm telling that you'll pay for that smart mouth. Count it, girl."

Amos tilted his head. He whispered, "Come on now. Whatcha doin'? No good awake like this, are you?"

Emme's daddy opened his mouth to speak, but then his throat locked up on him. He clamped his lips shut and tried to swallow down on the knot that threatened to cut off his airway. The corners of his mouth twitched a few times.

The Confederate flag behind him went still just in time for the sound of engine noise to carry to them again.

"What now?" Amos said a little louder. His eyes watered as he squinted against a pounding headache. It was worst this time so close to the previous effort. He thought he might pass out and hoped he'd fall away from the road instead of into it. "You gonna come when you're call now, hear?"

Emme's daddy closed his eyes and shuffled out onto the Stretch. He pulled his arms up into his ribs and bent his elbows like chicken wings. Amos giggled even though he could barely see at all. It was more than the tears. Black spots like gnats swarmed the edges of his vision and spread toward the middle of his sight.

The man leaned back like trying to shy away, but he clopped forward like someone was pulling him by his belly button with an invisible string.

Emme found her feet and skittered along the dirt up even with the bottom of her porch steps. She folded her arms up close to her sides in a way that looked a lot like her daddy in that moment.

A custom Canyon bore down like a metal monster crafted for this very moment. The matte black paint made it look fuzzy like it might not be real and its killing power only imagined. The front end lifted higher than the rear. Rich kids in town called that style the Carolina Squat, but Amos thought that nonsense was over.

"Do what you gonna do, old hoss. Get at it!" Amos screamed loud enough his voice broke on the second sentence.

The high grill above the over-jacked front shocks hit Emme's daddy in the ribs, shoulder, and head. He slammed to the street and was dragged under as the monolith of a vehicle locked up on its brakes and blue smoke boiled up from the tires. Before it came to a stop, Emme's daddy rolled under the tires, got dragged a little more, and then was spit out in pieces.

Emme screamed and Amos staggered. For a moment, he fully thought he'd called her out in the street on accident.

The half-jacked Canyon finally stopped in a smear of rubber and guts.

There wasn't much of the man left. What was there lay broken and twisted. Some dark part of Amos's soul knew he could drag the man back up into strange life, into some new form that would require a new name. A morbid curiosity, one that infects most children earlier than civil people like to admit, wanted to see what the bastard would become if Amos dared to reverse the process.

Emme let out another shriek and that awakened Amos's fading and drifting mind to what needed to be completed.

The door to the vehicle opened and a booted foot slipped out onto the high tilted running board.

Mr. Alabaster's mouth worked, showing bloody teeth. Bubbles formed and swelled from a long split along the flesh of his throat. As the blood bubbles popped, Amos expected words to fly out of them like in the cartoons, but whatever the man needed to say in his last words, they were lost.

"Alright . . . I'm only asking this once, so you better . . . ya best listen up." Amos's voice drew thready and old in his own throat. "Go down deep. And never find your way back. Eat the darkness and let it chew on you. Weep your black tears and gnash your bloody teeth with the worm that keeps on not dyin'. You hear? I said get!"

Emme's daddy went still like he was told. The stuff smeared along both lanes of the Stretch that Thursday was just meat with no spark of anything else left inside.

The door on the Canyon slammed and the truck tore away in a hurry, leaving blood, rubber, and acidic smoke. Two more doors opened and closed. There were only the two houses, so must have been one parent from each.

Amos knew exactly where he'd sent Alabaster and he sunk into darkness himself, not even knowing when he hit the ground.

The boy woke up to flashing blue and red lights. Night had settled and confused the line between consciousness and the lack of it. Emme leaned over him and kissed his sweaty forehead through the strands of hair stuck there.

That's how he was greeted back into the world.

He raised up slow with her help and saw his own daddy manhandling Dawg and Chicken away from the street where all the cops and folks dealt with the mess there. Amos had another thread of confusion pass through his aching mind. How come his daddy hadn't shook him awake to either deal with the animals or to just see if he were maybe not dead too? Why hadn't the cops checked on him? Maybe they had a couple beers together and decided all was fine.

"Come on," Emme said. "Run away with me."

Amos got to his feet and could only stagger for the first few steps, but then she took his hand and he started to run with her along the side of the road away from the houses. He had no idea in the dark which way they were going nor what might happen next. He wasn't clear on whether she meant to run away until the commotion settled or run away for good like hobos on a train.

Either way, they were alive, she had his hand and his heart, and all his power was for her.

Igloo Made of Flesh

ZOLTÁN KOMOR

MAYBE IT WASN'T such a great idea to save money on heating: returning home I discover that an Eskimo has built an igloo out of my family.

I rush into the kitchen, searching for something I can use against the arctic intruder, but the sight of blood makes me dizzy: Surpsingly, the Eskimo managed to use the 1200-watt Electric Kitchen Chef to grind my wife and four children into meat pulp, from which he made flesh-bricks for his hemispherical hut.

I don't have anything against foreign cultures and customs, but this is over the top. He even used up all the frozen beef from the refrigerator; maybe one family is hardly enough material for an orderly igloo.

I storm into the living room with a meat hammer. Nanook peeps out from the wet, sparkling, red cottage, and hides after seeing that my mouth is foaming with rage. I throw myself on my belly and crawl into the flesh cabin like a poisonous snake. He sits there, hiding his face between his kneecaps. As I raise the hammer, ready to strike, suddenly the pleasant warmth relaxes my cramped muscles. It penetrates my bones. I can literally feel the frozen marrow inside begin to thaw. I didn't realize how cold I was till now and almost forgot what heat feels like. I keep reminding myself, that I should smash the Eskimo's skull, but my anger steams out, like an evil djinn from a lamp, only the blessed feeling of warmth and safety remains, like I'm in my mother's womb again. Blood drips over my face from the meat-bricks as I crouch beside Nanook enjoying the blessed heat of this family nest. Staring out into my cold apartment from our body-warm cocoon I realize that the old saying is true: family is the warmth during cold moments.

Days pass. Sometimes I fondle the walls wondering if I'm touching one of my children's back, my wife's thigh, maybe minced beef, or just a mix of all of them. I try to recall the anger I felt when I realized my family had been slaughtered cold-bloodedly, but it's hard to be upset in this warmth, because heat is love itself. Only the faint smell of rotting meat reminds me what the igloo is made of.

I learn his name really is Nanook. Sometimes the Eskimo climbs out to hunt. He cuts a hole in the floor through which he catches the tenants below using a spear carved from a table leg. He turns on the Kitchen Chef, and builds the fresh meat pulp into the igloo. This is how our little shelter grows.

Soon we run out of neighbors, and without fresh meat, the walls turn cooler. We eye each other, wondering, how we could steal the other's body heat. But the civilized man rises in me: crawling out, stepping to the thermostat, sighing resignedly, I turn on the heat. The radiator clicks and soon the apartment grows warmer.

Nanook thinks spring arrived early. He wriggles out too, and sits quietly in an armchair. Soon the hut begins to rot. There's stink and lost love in the air. And the fear of a high gas bill, something Nanook wouldn't understand. Later, with a squelchy thump, the meat-cave collapses. I decide, I'll never try saving money on heating again.

WAR OF THE WILDFLOWERS

ARLO GOREVIN

REX KINDRED'S BIRTH went much as expected, except perhaps for the surprising detail that he was born with an inverted fishbowl instead of a head.

His mother was shocked at first, as there'd been no known history of cranial aquaria in her family, but as the midwife gently cleaned the last webs of bloody placenta from Rex's glassy skull and passed him into her arms, a tiny and vulnerable thing, Mrs Kindred felt nothing less than a surge of mother's love, the most complex and uncomplicated emotion of her entire life.

His father was perhaps less forgiving of the anomaly, at least in the beginning. He allowed himself a tough affection for the boy, as his own father had done for him, but there were times that he'd watch little Rex playing with his toy cars or building a tower from brightly-coloured blocks, and wonder how on Earth this had happened.

For his part, Rex was quite comfortable with his fishbowl head, because he'd never known anything different. In every other way, he was, as society would have it, a normal boy, and as he grew into a teen and then a man, the transparent sphere atop his narrow shoulders grew with him. The rust-coloured gravel that gathered where the glass was bonded to his neck, multiplied imperceptibly, always blanketing the bottom—or rather the top, as it was inverted—of the bowl. Initially, his mother had fretted about how to feed him, but a small garden of underwater plant life had blossomed from the gravel at birth, and the midwife had told Mrs Kindred that as long as Rex got plenty of sunlight, photosynthesis would provide all the nutrients he might need. The water within, which would grow cloudy over time but become clear once Rex had urinated, magically expanded its volume as he grew, always maintaining a level an inch or two below the top—or rather the bottom—of the glass orb.

His brain, as the many scans confirmed, was tucked into a little pink and white castle planted firmly upon the gravelly terrain. As he grew in body and intellect, the castle sprouted extra towers and turrets, the initially bland archway of its door evolving into rather a fetching portcullis. He could hear, after a fashion, explained to his parents as soundwaves travelling through the water, and he could communicate, either through sign language or, for the untrained, the pad and pencil he kept with him at all times.

But it was his vision that was, as even his father admitted, a wondrous evolutionary quirk. Two fish lived in the bowl, each an exotic collision of spines and fins, and *they* were Rex's eyes, relaying the world around him to his castle-bound mind via some unknowable wavelength. They would dart about the bowl when he was nervous, or drift serenely to the gravel when he was sleepy, or even duck behind the castle battlements when Rex was feeling shy, and almost everyone that ever met Rex thought they were quite charming. The fish were cyclopean, and people simply thought of their warm golden eyeballs as Rex's own.

And when he eventually left the small town he was born in and moved to the glittering metropolis of Velo City, he found people a little more wary but ultimately as kind and accepting of his differences as he was accustomed to. He got a job as a lifeguard at a popular swimming pool, where his acuity and flexibility of vision proved an asset. He could sit on his poolside podium and one of his fish could swim left, to keep watch on the group of children splashing near the faux waterfall, while the other could wriggle right to survey the old lady and the teen about to cross lanes in the deep end. It was an important, responsible role, and in the ocean-themed environs of the pool, all seaweed green tiles and mosaics of sharks and whales and jellyfish, his fishbowl skull didn't even seem that extraordinary.

He moved into an apartment in a part of the city that was equally as far from the poorest parts of town as it was from the richest, and made it as cozy as he could, painting the walls a cheerful, space-enhancing yellow and enriching his desk and bedside table with photographs of his parents. One of his co-workers bought him a coffee maker as a housewarming present, and they'd laughed at how the glass bubble of the pot resembled his head. It was such a thoughtful gift that Rex didn't even explain that he didn't need to eat nor drink.

He rarely saw his neighbours, bar the odd exchange in the hallway where he would tip his hat or incline his bowl in greeting. They seemed friendly, though not talkative, but still he kept his pad and pencil with him should it be needed, plus a laminated card to briefly introduce himself. There was a lady in the apartment next door, he gathered, though it was some time after moving in before he saw her. He heard her though, playing her TV at full volume long into the night, the water in his head vibrating as she yelled answers and curses at a quiz show, or cackled along with some sitcom's laugh track. The noise was an inconvenience, but Rex had been raised to live and let live, and so most nights he simply bracketed his head in soft pillows and tried to ignore the din.

The house back home had had a modest garden, and when Spring came around Rex found himself missing its little oasis of greenery, so he fixed a small window box to the sill outside his living room, and planted a handful of wildflower seeds in the soil. Tending to them became a part of his morning ritual, and soon enough they were a welcome explosion of colour. He had no way to smell them, of course, but he was quite sure the scent was delightful.

But one morning, as he drew back the curtains and opened the window, watering can in hand, he saw that something dreadful had happened. The pleasant bloom of wildflowers had been crushed, his window box a floral charnel house of torn petals and broken stems, the soil riven like a battlefield. Rex set the watering can down and leaned out to get a better look at the devastation. He picked up a petal, soft and silky between his fingertips, and wondered what on Earth could have happened.

Marauding birds? Possibly, although he couldn't imagine a quest for seeds yielding such vandalism. *Actual* vandalism? Unlikely, as his apartment was on the fifth floor, and he couldn't imagine what sort of person would go to the trouble of climbing. One of his fish fluttered right, to look at the corner of the building, and found no clue. The other swam left, to where the windows of his neighbours faced the street below as his did. Nothing, except . . .

Both fish converged at the left of his bowl, warm golden eyes narrowing as they fixed on the clot of soil that lay on his noisy next door neighbour's windowsill, arid and crumbling in the morning sunlight.

The window next door was raised, only a few inches, and from within Rex heard that throaty cackle again, joyful but unaccompanied this time, the laugh track unneeded.

He was due for a morning shift at the poolside, and so decided to leave any further investigation until later. As he opened his front door onto the hallway though he jumped, startled, his fish recoiling from the curvature of his bowl in surprise.

A woman stood before him, the tips of her slippers resting on the *Welcome* mat that Rex had placed outside his door. She was short and squat, enveloped in a voluminous pink dressing gown, her blunt, mottled features scowling at Rex from beneath a wiry nest of grey-black hair and a brace of untamed eyebrows. Cartoonishly large spectacles were perched on the bridge of her nose, big enough to pinch her nostrils. The frames were the same shape as Spiderman's eyes and behind the thick lenses, her own eyes were as dark as graveyard dirt.

In the stunted fingers of one hand, she held a broom, the fan of stiff straw-like bristles resting on the worn carpet of the hallway. One of Rex's eyes swam close to the gravel to get a better look, and he saw the clusters of soil still congealed amongst the bristles. A single red petal sprouted from the dirt, and all at once he understood what had happened to his window box.

"You!" The woman jabbed one stubby finger at him. "You, with your stupid glass head full of stones and fish! How dare you?"

As Rex understood it, his parents had been told that how he heard the world was something like how they themselves might hear with their head submerged in water, a chorus of muffled echoes. He supposed that was true, though of course he had nothing to compare his own senses with, but the woman's voice . . . it was whiny and rasping, as if she was speaking through her pinched nostrils *and* a throat full of phlegm. Its vibration scythed through the water in his head, and suddenly he imagined a wasp, born angry and thoughtless, buzzing endlessly and inexplicably delighted with its own annoying noise.

"Don't you know who I am?" the woman was demanding. "You should!"

You're my lunatic neighbour, Rex thought, but even as the notion bubbled from his brain-castle, the woman was introducing herself. She shook the broom with every syllable, dislodging soil from the bristles to tumble to the carpet.

"I. Am. Mrs. Verdigris."

Rex produced his laminated card. He held it out to Mrs Verdigris, who snatched it from his hand to peer at it through her lenses:

Hello.
My name is Rex. I'm afraid I cannot speak, but I am fluent in Global Sign Language, if that is convenient to you. If not, please let me know, as I have a pencil and pad at all times to communicate.
Best wishes
Rex Kindred

Mrs Verdigris shook her head as she read it, the lines flanking her sneer deepening. "Rex? What kind of name is that? Rex, like a dog?"

She threw the card at his chest, his fingertips catching it before it fell.

"Perhaps you *are* a dog." The woman spat. "I wouldn't be surprised. Hah! Whatever you claim your name is, I shall call you Fido."

He reached for his pocket, to fetch his pad and pencil, and Mrs Verdigris recoiled, raising the broom like a fighting staff.

"Don't you threaten me, you dog! I know you have a knife!" She thrust the bristles at his face. "You don't scare me. I know people, I write letters. Lots of letters!"

Slowly, Rex lowered his hands from his pocket. It was as clear as the water in his skull that there was no reasoning with the woman, at least not when she was in this state, so he stepped out into the hallway and closed his door behind him. He edged past her and headed for the stairs. As he started down them, he heard her shrieking after him.

"You're a freak, just like everyone else in this filthy city! You come here from God knows where, with your stupid fish eyes and pissy flowers! You're a freak, you hear me, Fido? A freak!"

He heard her all the way until he reached the lobby and opened the door, relieved when her rants were lost amid the morning traffic.

The confrontation with Mrs Verdigris weighed on him all that day, mostly because the random, blazing rage he'd seen in her was so alien to him. His parents had warned him about bullies from an early age, of course, fearful that his unusual nature would attract tormentors, and so he understood that such people existed, and also knew enough to feel pity for them rather than be intimidated.

She'd said the wildflowers smelled *pissy*, and while he doubted that, he still saw no sense in repeating the offence, but . . . he would *not* be afraid. He would simply fill his window box with other, hopefully more agreeable flowers. Spring was ending soon, so on his way home from work that day he bought some summer snapdragons, spider flowers, and purslane, already in bloom and ready to be planted. Arriving back at his apartment building he climbed the stairs, half-expecting Mrs Verdigris to still be there waiting for him, still in her dressing gown, still brandishing her broom.

She wasn't, but she *had* brushed the soil from the carpet onto his *Welcome* mat, stamping and grinding it into the fibres, all but obscuring the word. Rex's shoulders slumped at the sight, but he stepped over the mess and let himself in.

After dinner, as the evening grew cooler and darker, he opened his window and scooped out the destroyed wildflowers, replacing them in the soil with his new blooms. Some part of him considered staying up until morning to keep a wary fisheye on them, but of course he knew that was madness.

Instead, he slept, and dreamed fitfully of Mrs Verdigris, a

nightmare where she'd taken up residence inside the castle where his brain was cradled. She was using the handle of her dream broom to strike off coiled masses of his grey matter, then flipping the broom to sweep the fragments out onto the surrounding gravel. All the while, she cursed and complained, a rant expressed in angry little bubbles that rose to the top—or rather the bottom—of Rex's skull. In the dream, there was a *Welcome* mat outside his castle's portcullis, and Mrs Verdigris stamped his brains into it, her squat form quaking with every step.

He awoke early the next day, half-expecting to find that his window box had been attacked in the night, but thankfully all seemed to be well. He *was* tired though, and almost wished he could make use of his housewarming gift and sample the magical regenerative qualities of a coffee. Instead, he started his day with his usual stretching exercises, then moved to the bathroom to wash and shave.

When he'd mentioned his twice weekly shave to his co-workers, they'd been puzzled, teasing him good-naturedly about imaginary stubble. But as he'd explained, for him it was simply a balm, the equivalent of a relaxing bath or burning some incense. He did it because it was pleasant and brought back good memories.

When he was a boy, his father had been cautious about teaching Rex some of the more active pursuits that he himself had been schooled in as a child, wary that the ball games and the roughhousing might prove too dangerous for his son's glass cranium. Instead, they read stories together, and went for nature walks, and one day when Rex had walked in on his father with a face full of soap and a razor in hand, Mr Kindred had seen an opportunity for another father-son moment.

He'd shown Rex how to lather the brush and coat the lower half of his fishbowl in shaving cream, then handed him a razor with the blade removed, instructing him how to scrape the instrument gently against his glassy jawline (rinsing with cold water, of course, to prevent Rex's bowl steaming up).

Obviously, even as he matured, Rex never had the follicles to need maintaining, but twice a week he'd observe the ritual, grateful for its soothing simplicity.

An odd rasping sound from the living room made him pause. He set the razor down beside the basin and took a towel with him to wipe away the soap as he moved to investigate the noise. The towel fell from his hand as he came to his window and saw the broom, its fan of bristles scratching and scraping at the glass as it was thrust repeatedly at his window box. The broom dipped and wavered, angled as it was from Mrs Verdigris's window, but she'd already scored a couple of decent hits, uprooting some of the snapdragons and mashing a few of the purslane. Soil flew from the bristles, spattering against the pane.

Enraged, he strode to the window and wrenched it upward, his hands grasping at the broom. His fingers tangled in the bristles, but unseen, Mrs Verdigris yanked it away from him and took another swing at the spider flowers. Unseen, but he could hear her cackling.

He leaned further out of the window, swiping at the handle. He missed and stretched his torso out further. He was shirtless, caught mid-shave, and the rough wood of the frame scraped his flanks. He took another clutch at the broom and snagged it on an outward swing, pulling him a little further through the window.

Instinctively, one of his fish pressed itself to the lower half of his bowl, throwing a fearful glance at the street five floors below. The other fish swam left, and saw Mrs Verdigris tilting out of her own window, her stunted fingers locked around the broom handle. She was crowing with laughter, but above her glasses those feral eyebrows of hers were drawn together like thunderheads, her dull eyes furious. Her eyes widened when she saw Rex's torso as he angled himself through the window frame, his hand maintaining a precarious grip on the broom handle.

"You're naked!" she shrieked, and five floors below, passers-by paused to look up. "Naked as the day you were born! Pervert! Deviant! Beast of the field!"

It's just my shirt, Rex wanted to tell her, but now wasn't the time to fetch his pad and pencil.

"Peeerrrverrrt!" Mrs Verdigris bleated, that horrible, quavering voice resounding in Rex's skull. "First you plant those *pissy* flowers," she screeched. "Then you threaten me, and *now* you expose yourself! You're a monster! Bad dog! Bad dog!"

She jerked the handle from his fingers, arcing it back then swinging it forward again. Rex's fisheyes saw it sweeping towards his face and darted for cover behind his brain-castle. He couldn't deflect it, though; one hand was on the window frame to keep him from toppling out, the other flailing at air, and the spray of bristles slammed into the front of his head.

The impact snapped his skull back, his fingers unmooring from the window frame, and he stumbled backwards, his feet tangling. The water in his head churned, the bed of gravel rippling and rising. His legs flew from beneath him, the room tilting as he plummeted, landing hard on his back.

His head thumped against the carpet, the jolt a shockwave through the glass. One of his eyes was flung into the battlements of the castle, the other dizzied in a sudden whirlpool. The gravel swirled, and Rex's head was filled with the cacophony of a hundred tiny collisions. He would've screamed then, if he could.

When the tide finally settled some unknown minutes later, he very cautiously sat up, the fragments of gravel slowly sinking back into place like the flakes of a snow globe. One fisheye peeped warily over the turrets of the castle, then joined its twin at the curve of the bowl, each surveying the open window.

The broom was gone.

That lunatic, Rex thought fuzzily. *That bloody maniac. What the heck is wrong with her?* Carefully, he stood, feeling like his knees might unlock at any moment. From where he stood, he could see that she'd continued her attack on the window box; barely a single bloom remained intact. A stream of angry bubbles arose from his castle.

How dare she? He'd come to Velo City with no agenda but to make a life for himself, and this . . . this *harridan* had made it her business to project her own rage and unhappiness onto him. He wouldn't stand for it. He *wouldn't*. She was nothing more than a bully.

He dragged on a shirt, lest his *deviant nakedness* offend her, and grabbed his pad and pencil. His hands were shaking, but his scrawled message was clear enough.

LEAVE ME ALONE
WILL CALL COPS

LAST WARNING

He stormed out into the hallway and pounded on her door. He held his pad in one quaking fist, ready to thrust it at her mottled, jowly face, but as soon as his other hand knocked on the door, it swung inward, creaking with horror-movie ambience. He found himself facing the unlit hallway that led, like in his own apartment, to the living room.

He stood in the doorway for a moment, his hand raised for another strike on the door, unsure what to do. He settled for a modest tap on the door frame to further announce his presence, then started down the hallway.

Mrs Verdigris had photographs on her wall, each in a plain black frame, and while one fisheye fixed on the door that led to the living room, the other scanned the pictures, narrowing in confusion.

They were all monochrome, unfocussed, taken from some distance away.

They were all pictures of him.

Here he was the day he moved in, carrying a box of books into the building. There he was on the street outside, waving down a cab. Distressingly, here he was in work, sitting on his poolside podium. So many photographs.

At last he reached the living room. His grip had tightened on his scrawled note, crumpling it. Mrs Verdigris's window was still open, he saw, allowing in the drone of the morning traffic. As he drew closer, he saw that there were a few clusters of soil on the floor, most likely having fallen from the broom when she drew it back inside, and in sudden spite he stamped them into the carpet like brains into a *Welcome* mat.

There was a sudden breeze at his back, and an odd whooshing sound. The sound was annoying but brief, because in the next moment his skull shook with some great concussion, as if a depth charge had been tossed into his fishbowl. His eyes were driven into the gravel, his brain-castle shedding slivers of pink and white. Towers and turrets tilted in a watery maelstrom, and Rex fell to the carpet, stunned.

One of his fisheyes rose from the stones, blinking, and saw Mrs Verdigris above him, the broom raised.

"Bad dog!" she squawked. "Filthy Fido! Filthy beast!"

In desperation, Rex held his scribbled note out to her, but she struck it from his hand. The broom came down again, on his leg this time, hard.

"Look at the mess you've made, you pervert! Traipsing dirt into my lovely clean carpet! Deviant! Bad dog!" She jabbed the broom at his chest. "Dirt! Dirt everywhere, and now you begin to leak! *How fucking dare you?*"

Rex had been propping one arm beneath him, had been starting to stand, but he hesitated. What did she mean . . . *leak?*

And then came the sound, merely a tiny crackle at first, but seemingly louder than anything Rex had heard in his entire life. Beneath the crackle, a squeal was blossoming, the microcosmic song of glass particles kissing each other goodbye, and Rex's fisheyes widened as the hairline fractures began to spiderweb across the curvature of his head. There must have been more ruptures at the back of his skull, he realised, his water seeping out on to Mrs Verdigris's precious carpet, turning soil to mud.

More fissures splintered in front of his fishes, like frosted branches extending across the upper half of his head, and he started to rise, his hands cradling his skull. Through the branching cracks, he could see Mrs Verdigris smiling, her teeth as grey as wallpaper paste.

A terrible white scar zigzagged across his brow and a segment of his skull gave way, a vague diamond shape that itself split into two and tumbled to the carpet. Water gushed from the breach, more than he could stem with his hand. It rushed between his fingers, warm and tingling.

One of his fisheyes was caught in the tide, its tail flickering as it fought to escape, but to no avail. It was swept out in the stream, still struggling. Rex tilted his head to one side, tipping the remaining water away from the opening, and his other eye braced itself against a castle wall for safety.

Sensation flooded him. His brain shrank behind its battlements at the sudden chill, and without the acoustic sphere of the bowl, the world seemed filled with a deep, unending roar. Even in terror, his fisheye marooned on the carpet was still broadcasting to his brain on that unknowable frequency, and Rex saw Mrs Verdigris from two angles at once, horror in stereo. His fish at the castle wall saw her raising her foot, and the one on the carpet saw it descending with intimate inevitability.

Agony speared his every nerve as his eye ruptured beneath her weight. The organ relayed the world to him until the last possible moment, a carpet level view, the connection severing only after he'd seen a tangle of pale, greasy guts spew from its gaping mouth.

Mrs Verdigris said something, but for Rex there was only that endless roar, and he advanced upon her. She raised the broom, but he batted it aside. Blood plumed in watery clouds from his castle windows as his fingers sank into the meat of her throat, and his remaining fisheye swam through the veil to savour the moment.

Rex squeezed. Mrs Verdigris's tongue jerked from her mouth like some blind slug, her dull eyes bulging. She clawed at his hands, but Rex only tightened his grip, seeking her windpipe in the fleshy pillow of her neck. Her glasses jumped from her face, almost as if they'd been thrust from the bridge of her nose by her bloated eyes, and hung from one ear. She urinated, the piss soaking her slippers, and Rex kept throttling her, even as her pupils had frozen to empty gunshot wounds and her tongue had lolled from her mouth like that of a slaughtered cow.

Eventually, he stopped, because the strength seemed to be seeping from his arms and legs and the water in his bowl was almost completely fogged with red and he was so very *tired* now. He left her to slither down the wall and found a warm spot in the sunlight streaming through the open window.

Oddly, his senses seemed to be returning, very briefly, making a final cameo appearance before they shut down. The roar in his head began to quieten, usurped instead by the more prosaic sound of traffic in the street, and the magical chime of children's laughter. His remaining fisheye pressed itself to the glass to send one last signal before its wavelength dissolved into blackness, and strangest of all, before the world went dark Rex swore he could smell flowers.

A PIE-ON THE HOUSE

PATRICK WINTERS

SOMEONE WAS KNOCKING on Stan's door.

It didn't register with him at first—the knocking was coming in quick bursts, syncing up with Stan's strokes, lost against the groans coming in through his earbud. When the knocking became more pronounced, he figured whoever it was would eventually go away and leave him to his invigorating business. But when a few more raps followed, that hope went right out the window.

Stan gritted his teeth and groaned. He paused the video up on his computer. Brazzers' latest offering, *The Siege of Porktown*, would have to wait. And it was a damn shame, because the surrender of General Corn-Hole-is had been going so well.

He minimized the browser, plucked out the earbud, and stood up. He tossed his tissues onto the desk and thought about his great Aunt Dina.

Nothing and no one could wilt a raging boner quite like his late relative. The thought of her melted-wax face alone had been easing his most inopportune hard-ons ever since he was a teenager. He supposed he should have felt bad thinking of her in that way, especially now that she had passed, but frankly, it was the only time and the only way he'd *ever* thought about her in all his twenty-nine years. And since that wasn't broke, he wasn't about to fix it.

One more fleeting thought about those soggy kisses she used to give him put his Free Willy back into the icy waters. He gave himself an extra little adjustment, just to be safe, and headed for the front door.

He was certain that his face was red and scowling, but he didn't care if it was. He wanted whoever was still banging on his door to know that they were an intruding irritation upon his time and life. And if it was one of those holy-roller sorts, God or Allah or Xenu help them, because he was liable to go berserk on their superstitious asses. If there was anything more maddening to him than a hitch in the ol' Crank, it was when a bunch of idiots came around with whatever stupid brand of hoodoo they happened to be selling.

Stan stepped up to the front door and gave the knob a hard twist, swinging the door open. A delivery boy stood there in the hall, a square black carrying case in his hands.

"Good afternoon, sir." The kid's voice practically oozed out of his mouth, thick with congestion.

Stan didn't respond. He just leaned against his door and gave the kid a judging once-over.

The guy might have been in his early twenties. He sported one of those big smiles that straddled the line between cheerful and creepy, his off-whites on full display in a pudgy face whose skin was pallid and sweaty, looking sickeningly sleek under the fluorescent lights in the hall. There were shadows under his eyes—probably from late-night rounds of Dungeons and Dragons with the few friends he could scrounge up. A red cap sat on his head, a Moretti's logo stitched across it; he wore a matching vest that could barely cover the print of his Megadeth t-shirt, let alone the tubby gut beneath it. And there was a smell around the guy—a mix of mildew and the stink of community college debts.

"What the hell's this?" Stan said, nodding to the kid's case. "I didn't order anything from you guys."

The kid's smile didn't waver. "Not today, sir, but our records show that someone at this address put in an order for a pie last night?"

Stan squinted and tongued his cheek, his thoughts turning back to yesterday evening. It took a second or two, but it came back to him: yes, he *had* ordered out last night. After a couple of hours hanging with Mr. Bing-Bong, he'd worked up quite an appetite and called in for a supreme pie from Moretti's. But after an hour passed (and after a few more hits) he'd forgotten about it and ordered from Little Foshan, instead. The Chinese food showed, but the pizza never did.

"Yeah, right." Stan shrugged. "I guess I did. And I never saw or heard from you jerks. I sure as shit ain't paying for that now if that's what—"

"Absolutely not, sir!" the kid cut in. His voice tried to take on a respectful tone, but the lilt made it sound more like a parent patronizing their pouting child, and Stan didn't much care for it. "We had a little trouble at our store last night which prevented us from completing your order. On behalf of Moretti's, I'd like to apologize for the mishap; and to ensure our appreciation for your business, we'd like to give you your pie on the house—free of charge!"

The kid reached a hand into his case and pulled out an extra-large pizza box, a design of the Moretti mascot spinning a cartoon pie stenciled across its top. The kid's smile widened as he held the box out to Stan.

Stan accepted it with another shrug. "Sure. Thanks and all."

The kid gave a curt nod. "I hope you enjoy it."

He stood there a moment longer, his smile getting on Stan's nerves; then he turned, shuffling down the hall and out of sight as he turned the corner, heading for the elevators.

"Twerp," Stan grumbled.

He kicked his door closed as he turned about, heading into the living room. He slapped the pizza down on his coffee table and plunged onto his couch with a huff, his hormones quieted by the smells of cheese and olives that were setting his stomach to growling. The rest of General Corn-Hole-is' hard surrender would have to wait until later on, after a bite and some channel surfing.

Stan snatched up the remote and flicked his flat screen onto some re-run of *Bar Rescue*, then flipped the lid of the pizza up. Steam raised off the pie, looking fresh and delicious, the gracious toppings of Italian sausage, pepperoni, and peppers completely covering the face of the super-sized pie.

"Fucking excellent," Stan laughed. Maybe he'd have to call Moretti's and hope for them to fuck up more often, because he'd never gotten a pie from them that looked this damn good. He'd gladly accept some more apologies, if this is how they'd do it.

He pulled off a slice, fighting with the heaping helping of cheese that refused to let go of the rest of the pie. When the battle was won, he tongued the dangling mozzarella into his mouth and took a bite of the crust. Flavors erupted across his tongue, so strong and delectable that he had to wonder if free pizza really *did* taste better, like some people said; by the time he'd scarfed down that slice and gone on to another, he figured it must be true.

He leaned back and kicked his feet onto the coffee table, eating and laughing as John Taffer chewed out some googly-eyed bartender.

Time was running out for Stan.

His crappy old Bug was spitting and sputtering down the road as quickly as it could—but it surely wouldn't be enough to save his ass. The thirty-minute guarantee would be up any second, and if he was late—and if the customer called him out on it—Mr. Moretti would have his jewels. Literally. The old Italian chef had made his warning very clear, shouting it right into Stan's face before he'd left the store:

"You-a make sure this one's on-a time, or I'm-a gonna' chop off-a your balls and give 'em to my Momma to use in her Sunday night spaghetti!"

And Stan knew that he meant it. Now, where in the hell was . . . ?

He was out of his car and hustling up to the retirement home, where the delivery was to be made. He slammed through a pair of double doors and strode up to a reception desk, where a woman (who looked a lot like Bruce Willis, in an unconvincing wig and floral uniform) sat reading a magazine without pictures or words.

"I have a Meat Lovers special for a Dina Nolan!" he said, urgent and sweating, eyes scanning every which way for a clock.

"She's in Rec Room 2," the unsightly receptionist mumbled, turning another blank page of her magazine and pointing lazily to her right.

Then he was literally flying down the halls, rooms zooming past him, taking corners with his feet hanging above the floor.

He entered the spacious rec room, heaving breaths. He scanned the collection of senior citizens that were scattered about the blue-tinted room. Some wandered aimlessly, smacking into walls;

others sat in huge recliners, dozing—or maybe dead. Many of the ones that were awake and chatting with one another spoke in a language that sounded like Klingon. He was surprised to see his co-worker—the one who always wore Megadeth shirts and whose name he could never remember—standing in a corner, looking right at Stan and smiling that creepy smile of his. Stan figured he was here visiting a relative, but he had no time to ask the kid about it.

He swallowed down gravel. "Delivery for Dina Nolan!"

A few haggard faces looked over to him, but none answered. He repeated himself, and then a craggy voice struck up in response.

"Dina! Dina, you old bitch! Your pizza's here!"

Then he was standing in front of two women, each sitting in chairs, one awake and shaking the arm of the other, who wasn't. This second woman wasn't only out—she was gone. Long gone. She was a rotting corpse, her skeletal body wrapped in a faded pink robe with dust and cobwebs all over it, her parchment-skin hands lying lazily over the armrests and her emaciated face lolling upwards, her gray-streak head lying over the headrest.

"Dina!" the other woman shouted in a vulture's voice. "Your Meat Lovers is here!"

The corpse gave a jolt and a cough, shooting out dust from her shrunken lips. She opened her clouded eyes and looked up to Stan, smiling with feeble pleasure, a patch of skin splitting at her right cheek and lilting off her face like a leaf on a branch.

"Ahhh—meat, you say!"

She slowly rose up in her seat, a tongue the color of a dried dog dropping playing at her lips. Hokey porno music started playing from somewhere in the room, with its funky 70s beats and bow-chicka-wow-wows.

"I love me some meat! Give it up, sonny!"

Stan looked down at the box in his hands, confused at how he was suddenly holding it, the box slanting and pressed up tight against his crotch. And there was warmth down there, almost as if . . .

The lid of the pizza box flung open, and Stan screamed, seeing that his Little Stan was sticking out through holes in both the box and the pizza, and that his member had been burnt by the heat of the pie, his skin red and raw—at least, wherever it wasn't blackened and scorched.

The corpse in front of him gave a moan of anticipation. "Extra sausage!"

Dina Nolan leaned forward in her chair, inching her face up to the pizza and his crotch, her mouth drawing open further and further with every word. "Just . . . the way . . . I like it . . ."

And then her mouth was around him, her dried tongue like sandpaper against his burnt buddy, her cracked teeth chomping down and her dusty throat swallowing. He screamed again in agony and revulsion . . .

Stan woke up hacking, his stomach giving threatening lurches, a burning sensation welling up in the back of his throat.

He pulled himself off the couch, stumbling through the early-evening dark and shaking the sweat-drenched hair out of his face. He went for the bathroom as quickly as he could, feeling like a well-shaken beer whose tab was about to be popped.

He dashed into the bathroom and arched his back, thrusting his head toward the toilet as he hurled. A stream of gunk and *blech* came out of him, splashing into the porcelain with the sound of a wet mop smacking a floor. He shuddered, trying to catch his breath before another, smaller rush of stomach contents came out.

He groaned, spitting out that awful taste in his mouth as he steadied himself, trying to calm the bubbling of his gut. He felt clammy all over. And his shirt was clinging to his torso, sopped through with sweat.

After another uncertain moment, he righted himself. The water and his vomit swirled away as he flicked the toilet's handle. He gave a lowly snort, fighting back against a swell of congestion, then turned around, planning to head for his bedroom and switch out shirts.

But then his stomach rumbled, clenching up on him, and he knew what was coming next.

He threw himself at the toilet, sliding his pants off and plopping down just in time for the hot torrent that came shooting out of him.

His bowels took the wheel and drove for the next few minutes.

The rest of Stan's night would go on to be the most miserable one he'd ever had—aside, perhaps, from the time he got wasted with some buddies on a trip into Mexico, drank three whole Pachucan Sucker-Punches, and woke up in a barn the next morning, a mile off from where their shitty little hotel had been. But at least the Mexico ordeal had provided some entertainment before the vomiting and the shits kicked in on the dreaded "next day;" last night, it'd just been the vomiting and the shits.

He was up and down all night long, stuff either coming up or blasting out of him every other hour, becoming a proverbial elevator shaft that his bodily fluids insisted on using. Chills were always sweeping over him, despite the fire sparking underneath his skin; there was no question about it—he had developed a whopper of a fever and in no time at all. Add a dizzy head to the matter, and it was enough to ensure that he wouldn't get a moment's rest all night long. The best he could manage were some half-in, half-out bouts of semi-consciousness, when his thoughts drifted between self-pity and things that weren't quite dreams, but which certainly weren't coherent notions, either. A doctor would call it delirium, but Stan's prognosis was that it just plain fucking sucked.

One thing came to him pretty clearly though, and he stewed in the idea all through the night, when he could manage the effort: it had been that damn pizza from Moretti's that made him sick. Something had been wrong with it, and it was playing hell with him now. Maybe the veggies had gone bad, or the meat was spoiled, or maybe the cheese had originated from the teat of a diseased cow. He wasn't sure if such a thing were possible, but he definitely knew this: there'd been a price to pay for free pizza, after all.

He'd eventually passed out on the couch sometime after dawn, too weary to stay above the wake of cognizance any longer. He stayed that way until his cell phone roused him, vibrating along his coffee table and playing "Body Talk" by Ratt.

Stan cracked his eyes open and moaned. He shoved himself off his side with a great deal of effort and pulled his blanket tighter around himself. He bobbed, as though he were in a dingy cast out to sea. He let out a deep, sickened burp, the meaty reek of it wafting up and smacking him across the face.

He groaned as he leaned forward, reaching for his phone. He

gave a vindictive smack to the Moretti's box that was still on the table; a few pieces of the damned pizza remained, the smell of them reaching his nostrils and making his stomach gurgle dangerously.

His fingers fumbled around his phone for a second before he flicked it on.

"Hell—o?"

An officious voice answered. "Hello, mister . . . Nolan?"

Stan grumbled a confirmation.

"This is Vince Smithers. I'm the manager of your local Moretti's Pizzeria."

Stan's anger cut right through his nausea like a cannonball through fog. His stomach gave another churn, but his head became a little clearer as the manager continued on.

"I'm calling in regard to the pie you ordered the evening before yesterday, and which our store regretfully failed to deliver. I wanted to personally apologize for that failure and for any inconvenience it may have caused you, but you see—"

"What you should be apologizing for is poisoning me," Stan cut in. Another warm surge of bile tickled at his throat; he forced it back down with a shudder. "I ate your god-damned complimentary pie, and I've felt awful ever since!"

The manager guy went quiet for a moment, chewing on that. "I'm sorry, sir, but I'm not sure what—"

"*Your. Pie.* I should fucking sue you people. I'm just glad I didn't eat all of it, or I'd probably be hospitalized by now. Still might—" he paused, tossing a belch away from the phone "—have to be . . . "

"I'm sorry, sir, but you're not making any sense . . . "

"Would it make sense to you if I bring what's left of your garbage pizza down there and shove it down your *god-damn throat*?"

The guy was slow to respond again. "Sir, are you trying to tell me that you received a pizza from us within the last twenty-four hours?"

"I got something from you fucks, but I'm not so sure if it was pizza. Maybe the Black Plague special—"

"Sir, I assure you that's impossible. No pizza was ever delivered to you on our behalf, and that's why I was calling you—to settle up with you about the matter. You see, there was an incident the other night that involved your order."

Stan felt another urge to up-chuck, but he fought against it, his confusion trumping his queasiness.

"Your order was on its way when our delivery boy . . . had an accident. I'm afraid he drove his car off the Stetson Bridge and into Jackson Bend. He didn't survive." The manager paused and then spoke in a quieter tone, sounding uncertain—perturbed. "Police have been saying it . . . might have been on purpose. Ethan *had* been acting strange lately. Well, stranger . . . "

The manager got back to his official tone. "As I was saying, the incident was a shock to our store, and we hadn't had an opportunity to reach out to you about the matter until now. Now, you say you received a pizza from somebody? Might I ask that you describe them? Maybe one of my employees already saw to this matter, but I have no record of it. I simply can't imagine—"

"The kid was young," Stan said; if he didn't get this call done with soon, he'd be barfing onto his phone. And judging by the groan of his gut, he might be needing a change of underwear, too. "Tubby. Pale. Wearing your guys' uniform—and a Megadeth shirt."

There was a stretch of silence on the other end of the line. "That's not possible, sir."

"Fuck possible!" Stan shouted, instantly regretting the effect it had on his gullet. He reached a hand out to the pizza box on the table, smacking it and sending the lid flying up. "I've still got some of—"

He stopped, gagging at the sight of the leftover pizza.

The last three pieces had not only gone bad—they hardly looked like food anymore. It was all mushy, the pieces merged in a wet, disgusting lump that smelled strongly of algae and shit. Bits of grass and a few dead little pollywogs clung to the pizza and the inside of the box, which now looked crumpled and absolutely soaked through with water.

It was too much for Stan. He hurled, dropping his phone onto the couch as his vomit went splattering onto his legs. There were a few remaining chunks of nearly-digested bread and cheese in the copious mix, but there were other things, too—round, gray globs that looked an awful lot like . . . fish eggs.

Another rush of vomit shot out of him, and at the same time, he felt a wet slosh filling up his pajama bottoms and spreading along the couch. But it wasn't warm, as one would expect; it was chilled, freezing—like the water of a lake on a January morning. And whatever the stuff was, it just kept coming out of him, just like the rush of sick erupting from out of his gut, the vomit going from a muddy brown to a stark and strange gray, the consistency becoming clearer and more fluid with every expulsion.

Stan went into convulsions as the onslaught of gunk kept spilling out, his eyes rolling up as he trembled, trying to scream, only to choke on the awful slop.

He flopped down onto the floor, gyrating about in the awfulness he'd expelled, his clothes soaking it up and his skin becoming slick with it all. He could just barely hear the static rasp of the Moretti's manager shouting out for his attention on the phone, his repetitions of "Mr. Nolan?" becoming background noise against Stan's retching and quivering.

A few fleeting thoughts passed through Stan's mind as he twitched on the ground: the idea of calling an ambulance; a wish that he could make it through whatever this was; an image of that smiling delivery boy, saying how he hoped that Stan enjoyed the pizza.

And then Stan went still.

THE PEOPLE AROUND YOU

LUCY LEITNER

Ugh. Why is there a positive relationship between bathroom floor water levels and cocktail prices? Do the other patrons really think a lack of legit happy hour specials entitles them to flood the bathroom?

Those punk bars we said we grew out of, their facility walls may be covered with graffiti, but we didn't have to wade through a pool of grimy, mystery liquid to use them. It's not like I didn't want to get out of here and back to the table as quickly as possible. Kacey was in the middle of a story that could be life changing. Tim and Chloe seemed to have hit it off. Call me a matchmaker. A decade of friendship with both of them and somehow they hadn't met until this outing at a hip, new rooftop bar that promised the social experience of the 21st century. Whatever that meant.

Twenty seconds of hand washing? Eh. Ten will do. I rub my hands under the dryer. If only they had one for my boots. I shake what I hope is just water off the soles and push open the door.

"What'd you drown in there?" The woman shoves past me into the single-stall restroom, slamming the door shut before I have a chance to defend myself.

"Almost." Who talks to another human like that in real life, with their real face, without hiding behind a username and a cartoon profile pic?

It's darker than when I left, the setting sun casting a reddish glow on the rooftop revelers. Jeez, the angry woman can't be right, can she? No. Unless my phone is lying, I've been in there two minutes. Must be that time in the evening when a quick trip into the restroom looks like hours passed in the sky. Or maybe time is just flying on this rooftop as it does with good friends, conversation, and martinis.

"Oh, Lauren, listen to this." Kacey doesn't wait for me to sit. She'd been holding back her big news until I returned. The new client that was going to make the branding agency she founded. "Get ready for this."

"I'm ready. The client is?"

"You can't change the people around you." She pauses, stares into my eyes. "But you can change the people around you."

Huh? My look must have conveyed that sentiment because she says, "Did I just blow your mind?"

"Uh no. That's a viral fad. I've seen like twenty videos of people saying that in the past week. Hell, I even posted one."

"You can't change people," Chloe says. "I wish we could. I'd change the white supremacists. I have no tolerance for intolerance."

"That still makes you intolerant." Tim glares at Chloe while he stirs his old fashioned like a Bond villain petting his hairless cat. Sure, Tim and Chloe would have none of the same letters in a personality test, but that's kind of why I thought they'd hit it off. Yeah, Tim can be difficult—why else would he need a friend to set him up?—but the outright hostility is new. What happened when I was in the ladies' room?

"So, Kacey, the new client you were going to tell us about." Maybe changing the subject will lessen the tension.

"Oh yes," Kacey says. "But first, martini." She picks up the glass and smiles for an invisible photographer. "Friday vibes!"

"Sure, but who is the client?"

"Oh, it doesn't matter who it is," Chloe says. "I just want it to be known that I'm so proud of my friend for growing her agency. I'm just so proud."

"I'm not sure who needs to hear this, but—" Kacey says.

"Nobody. Nobody needs to hear whatever nonsense is gonna spew out of your mouth," Tim says. His hand clenches around his lowball glass, the knuckles turning white.

"Well, I wanna hear who the client is."

"Oh, this is a huge client. Life changing. Major reveal coming!"

"It's a company that I can support, right? It matters to me to only support brands that align with my values," Chloe says.

"What values? The ones that shift as much as your fat ass on that stool?" Tim says.

"Tim, what is your problem? That doesn't even make sense," I say.

"Can you listen to these two self-important twats anymore?"

"Actually, no. I'm a little confused, guys. You don't talk like this, Kacey. I'm your friend, not your Instagram follower. Tell me about the client."

"Lauren, drop me some love. I've been digging deep."

"Deep into daddy's wallet to start that bullshit agency."

"Tim, quit being an asshole!"

"I stand with Kacey," Chloe says.

"I so need another appletini," Kacey says. "I need it like yesterday."

"Of course that's how a selfish bitch like you would use time travel." Tim takes a sip from his drink, spits it across the table. It doesn't reach Kacey. She's too busy trying to see her reflection in her empty martini glass to notice. What is wrong with Tim? Did Chloe say something to him while I was gone? Are my matchmaking skills really that rusty?

"I do not tolerate misogynistic language," Chloe says.

"OMG guys, this appletini is a literal game changer. I don't feel drunk at all."

"Jesus, Kacey, I wish you were. Please come back to Earth." What was that about changing the people around me? Please bring my friends back! The people I left to use the restroom, not these . . . avatars I returned to.

"She's just taking up air, air that should belong to someone with something original to contribute," Tim says. He's shaking, the veins popping in his forearms from clenching the glass and in his neck from speaking through gritted teeth. Like he's holding in something terrible about to be unleashed. What in the hell happened when I was in the bathroom?

"Just to set the record straight, I do not believe in air hogging under any circumstance," Chloe says.

"Then you should stop yapping, you self-righteous shrew!" The lowball glass in Tim's hand shatters. Blood gushes from his palm. He shoves the glass shards into Chloe's face, twists his wrist, and pulls his hand away. Blood drips out of her eyes, down from her cheeks, and pools on the table.

"Oh, it's real right now," Kacey says.

"It's gonna get a lot realer," Tim says.

Chloe smashes her margarita into the table. She picks up the now pointy stem of the glass. Tim dives off his stool as it plunges into his shoulder.

"Bitch!" From the ground, he kicks the table. It collapses on Kacey's lap. Martinis spill and glass shards slice her bare legs.

"Stop it! Both of you!"

"You do not tell me what to do," Tim growls from the floor. His bloody hand wraps around shattered glass and he throws it at me. A shard hits my arm. It feels cold. It takes a couple seconds for the bleeding to start. What it lacks in pain it makes up for in blood. "Who are you to tell me to stop anything?" He lifts himself back to his feet, snarling. A face I've never seen before. Who is this troll who lurks within Tim?

"Kindness matters!" Chloe screams as she lunges into Tim, knocking him back onto the ground.

"Blood *balayage*," Kacey says, combing her bloody fingers through the ends of her blond hair. "That's a thing, right?"

"Ermahgerd yes!" The woman at the table behind us says. "Totally digging that look." She grabs my bleeding arm and I rip it away. She runs her fingers through her brown curls, and now the ends just look a little wet. Another victim of influence.

"Beat that bigot and rip his tongue out so he can't say another bigoted thing again!" someone shouts.

The tables around us are empty. The whole rooftop has encircled our party, watching. If I were them and on the periphery, I would run. It's like they're salivating, watching Chloe pull at Tim's shirt, shrieking, "I do not stand with your hate!"

She scrapes a piece of glass into his cheek, and he grabs her wrist, rolling her onto her back. He straddles her, slams her head into the ground.

A cacophony of voices, some shrill, some angry.

"Yeah, shut that banshee up!"

"I do not believe in this."

I grab Tim by his shoulders, pulling him back, but his hands remain on Chloe's head and when he shakes me off, he lets her head drop to the ground. And she doesn't resist anymore.

"Someone help me!" I keep pulling. No one comes to my aid.

"Don't worry, I'm recording all of this," another unfamiliar voice shouts.

"Kacey?"

"I'm just here living my best life," she says.

"You don't deserve to have a life," Tim says, his sneer focusing on Kacey.

"Yeah!" someone, a patron or the bar staff, shouts from the crowd that surrounds us. A woman shoves through the crowd to Kacey, beer bottle in hand.

"Oh, thank you. Help me hold him back." I dig my nails into Tim's shoulder, pulling him away from Kacey. "Come on, help me!"

The woman rolls her eyes, smashes her beer bottle over Kacey's head, and before I can even move, slits my friend's throat. It's not like my arm. The blood gushes immediately. Kacey grasps at her neck, but the seeping blood makes it too slippery, and it just keeps flowing. She falls out of her stool, landing on Chloe. My friends bleed to death on the rooftop floor. The crowd stares at them, some smirking with satisfaction that these people they don't know got what they deserved. Some are in shock, at least that's what they're projecting. A single tear falls from the eye of a chubby man.

Tim turns to me. I don't wait to hear what vitriol will come out of his mouth as I shove through the circle of strangers. I'm going to the only place that makes sense. Thank god it's unoccupied. I slam the single-stall bathroom door behind me and lock it. Silence. No banging at the door. No screaming. Nothing. Just a slight sloshing. It doesn't matter what it is anymore.

I run water over my arm in the sink. The wound isn't deep and I still can't feel it. Maybe it's the shock. Maybe it's the relative respite. This is where I was before everyone lost their minds and turned into some cowardly cartoon versions of people they want to pretend to be, or maybe who they really are. But is Kacey, she of the master's degree and her own business, really little more than the vapid spouter of social media cliches? Is Chloe no more than a collection of all the moment's right opinions? Is Tim secretly murderous?

The blood washes down the drain, the water becoming pinker until it runs clear. The bleeding stops. How long have I been in this room? My phone is in my bag at the table. I can't stay in this bathroom forever. This is where I was before everything went to Hell. Please, let opening this door return me to reality.

It's twilight on the rooftop bar. The tables are filled with friends and colleagues sipping their troubles away. Tim, Chloe, and Kacey are smiling at the high-top.

"Jeez, Lauren, you've been in there forever," Chloe says. "The suspense about Kacey's new client is killing us."

"Guys, listen to this," I say. "You can't change the people around you. But you can change the people around you."

Blank stares.

"Did I just blow your mind?"

THE SACK CUTTER

NIKKI NOIR & S.C. MENDES

"I DRIVE MARVELOUS people to marvelous places in a marvelous way."

From the backseat, Johnny looked at the rearview mirror. "Come again?"

The driver's sparkling green eyes connected with his briefly, then returned to the road. "You're Johnny Troutman, right?"

"I am." Johnny hadn't expected recognition today, but he was always ready for a fan. He flashed his camera smile. "Is that part of your S—"

"S.P.A. Routine? Heck yes, sir! *'See it. Prepare for it. Affirm it'*. I submerge myself in S.P.A. daily. And . . . " She pulled a notecard from her inside her suit jacket pocket. "I practice the 'Be-Do-Have' method for each of these affirmation goals. Which I recite three times a day, too."

"I'm impressed . . . Claire," he said, looking at the driver details on his phone app. Johnny leaned to the side for a better view of the woman, realizing he had ignored almost every detail as he hopped into the Uber and gave a rehearsed greeting. At only 150K subscribers across platforms, Johnny was able to afford a luxurious life while rarely running into his followers day-to-day.

After the mechanical *hello*, Johnny dived into his phone for the flight itinerary, assuming this was just another ride-share crap car and basic driver. Now though, his fingers slid over the seats, appreciating the immaculate leather of the Lexus. There were even bottles of water in the seat backs. The woman was quite attractive, too.

"Seems like you're finding success with my content . . . "

In the rearview mirror, a smile exploded across Claire's face. "Heck yes!"

"Oh good. Otherwise this could have been an awkward drive."

They both chuckled.

"I don't see how anyone *couldn't* find your teachings helpful. Don't get me wrong. It's difficult at first to form new routines and thinking patterns. You want to give up. At least I know I did. I wanted to quit soooo badly. But you gotta keep faith and keep hustling and your best life really does manifest." Her voice started to quiver, like a shoddy beaver dam about to break. "I . . . You can't imagine what things were like for me . . . You changed my life. Saved me."

Claire was talking a mile a minute, so Johnny just smiled, waiting for her to get all the emotion and thoughts out. He found it best to let women talk without interruption. Especially when they were praising him.

"I'm sorry," she said. "You must be like *who's this crazy Uber driver?* I bet you get this kind of *fan-girl-thing* every day. You don't need it from me. I'm sorry. My lips are sealed till we get to the airport."

"Don't apologize." Johnny waved it off with his hand. "I'm honored my work has had such a positive impact on your life. Thank you for allowing me to serve you."

"And I you. When this is all over, I hope you'll honestly rate me so I know if there's anything I can improve."

"Improve? This Lexus is beautiful. You have water bottles for passengers. The temperature is ambient. Everything's perfect. Or should I say marvelous."

"Always overdeliver, right?"

"In my experience, I've found that's the way to go. Keep giving and eventually you'll manifest your big break."

"I think I just did," Claire whispered so low he almost didn't hear it.

"What's that?"

"Positivity gurus get a lot of flack. Same as Multi-Level-Marketing like Mary Kay and Herbalife. But it really works. Today proves it. When you sat down, I went from 99% certain to not a

shred of doubt that the universe listens. Sorry, I'm rambling again."
Her face blushed and her hand went to the glove box. She passed
him back a flyer. "You. The timing. Everything. It may seem silly,
but when else am I gonna have a chance to show off my big dream
to the man who inspired me to change."

"*Limos and Ladies*?" Johnny read the front of the color
advertisement. "Clever name."

"I went from depressed drop-out to marvelous Uber driver thanks
to your motivational content. And now I'm gonna be my own boss.
No more driving. I bought four limos. Hired four accident-free ladies.
And I couldn't have done it without you. Five-minute manifestations.
Vision boards. Goal setting. Hustle. I bought it all and it finally paid
off." She took a deep breath and let out a satisfied sigh. "I launch on
Monday. Today is officially my last day driving for Uber. And of all
people, Johnny Troutman is my final fare." She giggled. "And people
still think there are things like luck and coincidences."

"Everything happens for a reason," Johnny agreed, shifting in
his seat so she could see more of his winning outfit in the mirror.
"Sounds like you and I have similar beginnings. Depressed and fed
up with life. And now . . . we see the light and receive our blessings
from the universe."

"I know the reason. It's so I can thank you. Return the favor."

A glossy film of tears threatened her eyes, and now it was him
fighting to keep the grin from overtaking his face. This was the kind
of chick he could have eating out of his hands. She'd already
swallowed his seed deep and was no doubt vomiting hustle-culture
cliches and Instagram quotes all day long.

I wish I could . . .

Even if he was willing to postpone his flight, all pussy except
Lindsey's was off limits. That was part of the promise to himself until
this business venture ended. Especially a young woman like Claire.
Banging a die-hard follower would damage his brand and future
business. That's why he had Lindsey. He prayed she lasted two more
years. By then, he would be thirty-five and would have made enough
money to retire from the Guru game. But already he worried the
sights in Vegas would make Lindsey look like yesterday's leftovers.

"Well, from the bottom of my heart, you're welcome." He bowed
to the rearview mirror.

"How rude of me. I should be asking about you. What marvelous place are you off to? An amazing conference, I'm sure?"

"If I were, I would offer you front row tickets to show my appreciation. But alas, I'm off to Michigan to check on my goddaughter. After my sister passed, I've been doing what I can to make sure Evelyn has a positive adult male influence in her life."

"That's beautiful. So much cooler than a dime-a-dozen conference for entrepreneurs. You really are an amazing guy."

There was definitely a suggestive tone. Damn. She probably was open to a quick and secretive fuck. Still, he couldn't risk it. He could use the niece-lie and keep Claire as an iron in the fire for the future. Johnny never posted his real life to social media. And it wasn't likely his 150K subscribers would see him at the MGM Grand for the fight. This way, if Claire still idolized him once he hung up his career hat *and* Lindsey, she could be a wonderful fling. But at the moment, sex with the young, seductive Uber Driver was a no-no.

He'd probably cut his trip short after the fight. Head home to Lindsey to squash these desires springing up. It was the whole unspoken point of their relationship. He provided her a cushy life and she fulfilled his sexual fantasies and kept quiet.

Get me off, so I don't get myself in trouble with groupies.

"Since I can't offer you conference seats. Here's the next best thing." He took a card from the special divider of his card case. The cards for 'irons'. "Next time you're in Houston and you have time, text me and we'll meet up for lunch. I'll need to hear all about the success of *Limos and Ladies*."

He leaned forward with the card as the car stopped at a red light. Claire turned to take it.

Then he lost consciousness.

"You're back." The chipper voice vibrated the base of his skull, exacerbating the pain already seeping into his head.

Johnny blinked a few times, adjusting to his surroundings, though there was not much to see. He was in a bare room, cold, and on a bed.

"Uh . . . " *The airport. Uber. That voice.* "Claire?"

"You remember my name!" She stood over him now, sporting another wide smile. Her generic chauffeur outfit was gone and a black *apron* hung from her neck. "But do you remember *who* I am?"

"You were driving. What happened? Car accident?" Johnny attempted to shield his eyes from the overhead light for a better look but couldn't move.

"I safely deliver clients where they need to go. For four years, I saw that goal in my mind's eye, prepared for all my success, affirmed my spotless driving record. I don't get into accidents; not in my reality."

"That's great but—wait, what the fuck?" He looked down to find his wrists tied to something under the bed. A corset was pulled tight against his bare chest. Although his shirt was missing, Johnny was still clothed in his pants, socks, and shoes.

No, I'm hallucinating. I hit my head. This is a dream—

"Relax," Claire said, pulling up a chair and sitting next to the bed. "Don't put yourself in a *vibration of fear.*"

"Where am I?"

"A secret place the universe showed me."

"Not funny, Claire. Why am I tied up?"

"So you can't get away."

Before, there had been confusion, concern over the unknown. Johnny assumed there would be a logical explanation for the misunderstanding though. Now, her words squashed any hope of that. The pain in his head vanished and Johnny's attention narrowed to survival.

"Claire," he said, fighting to keep his voice calm, trying to remember crisis techniques from his psychology training. "Please help me understand what's going on. One minute we're in your car, exchanging marvelous ideas, and now this."

"Don't judge the experience, Johnny. Accept it as part of the reality you manifested. Your desire."

"That *I* manifested? Claire . . . you're kidnapping me."

"You know that's not how life works."

"Claire, I did not want this," Johnny said, keeping his voice firm but calm. "I wanted a ride to the airport. I wanted to go to—"

"There are no accidents. Your subconscious mind wants this even if your conscious mind doesn't. That's why we attracted each other today. I wanted to thank you and deep down you want someone to save you from yourself, the double life, the lies."

"Save me?" His exterior cracked and Johnny flopped on the bed, pulling against the ropes binding his wrists.

"I saw your flight itinerary. You weren't going to Michigan."

"Who cares where the fuck my plane was going."

"You really need to relax. In this vibration the—"

"Don't tell me what to do!"

"Fine." Claire held up her hands. "You're the guru."

"Help! Somebody!" Johnny strained to lift himself from the mattress, seeing the open door behind her, hoping his words would find their way outside to waiting ears.

"You should know that isn't going to help. This cabin is almost to the Sabine Forest. Miles of nothing but lush trees." Claire produced a long butcher knife from the pocket of her apron.

Seeing the blade, Johnny suppressed the anger and fear boiling in equal measures. She was insane, and if he was going to stop her from using the knife, he needed to get his emotions under control.

Johnny breathed as best he could remember from all the yoga and meditation techniques he touted to followers but didn't practice himself.

"You're right, Claire." Johnny said, his confident façade slipping back in charge. "I must want this. Help me understand how we can fix this?"

"Well, we need to identify the problem first. You still don't know who I am, do you?"

"Please understand. I meet marvelous people like you every day. I can't remember everyone. I savor the moment I spend with them in whatever capacity that is—dinner, a ride to the airport, someone fixing a broken appliance in my home—and then I must move on."

"I'll give you some hints. I'm not a native Texan. I'm an MCC Thunderbird. Well, I was. Never graduated—say didn't you go to Mesa Community College?"

"No," he said, mentally rewinding the years to formulate a response. "But, I did work near the MCC campus. Those are my roots. It was at a real rundown bar. But like you, I'm somewhere much happier now. I set goals. Visualized. Acted as if. Affirmed it. And manifested my best life. How coincidental we both ended up here in Texas."

"Everything happens for a reason." Her voice was flat and chilling. "*Uncle Monkey's* wasn't that miserable, was it?"

At the mention of his former campus bar employment, the corset felt like it contracted. Was she a psycho fan stalker who knew every aspect of his life or was she a customer when he tended bar there? Maybe he shouldn't have said 'rundown'.

"You know *Uncle Monkey's*? Cool. Maybe you could untie me, and we could talk about the place." Johnny chuckled nervously. He could still salvage this situation. Now that he was calm again, there was a chance for negotiation.

"No, you're right. *Uncle Monkey's* was rundown. An unhappy place with unhappy drunks. Easy grounds for smooth talking bartenders to con a sad confused freshman."

Oh, shit . . .

Confused freshman. Sadly, that didn't narrow down Claire's identity, but it did reveal *how* she knew him. Before he entered the field of personal development, Johnny's passion was bartending and sport fucking. From the moment he left his parents' house until his twenty-sixth birthday, nineteen-year-old *freshies* like Claire weren't individuals to Johnny. There were his M.O.

Anywhere he went, he found lonely, broken females, and they flocked to his voice. When he decided to use his natural charm and oratory skills to increase his accumulation of wealth instead of pussy, he joined the hustle culture and growth mindset cult of personal development. The new career was a guaranteed money maker, and even though he had a new persona and stage name, Johnny was aware his past, if discovered, could pose a potential problem. It's why he didn't want the status of Tony Robbins or Chucky V. There was almost no escape from that level of fame.

Leading with this past weakness in mind was part of his marketing plan to proactively deal with any hot water *if*—when—that day arrived. He never claimed to be a saint in any of his courses. And although Johnny remained silent on the specific addictions and problems of his youth, in all content referring to his past and how he rose to manifesting wealth, health, and happiness, he simply alluded to overcoming *personal demons* through the daily S.P.A Routine and his Be-Do-Have method.

Over the last two years, his popularity grew, and he continually reminded himself that it wasn't illegal to be a womanizer. All the girls he'd bagged back then were over eighteen and had consented. He did nothing wrong. His actions were frowned upon, sure, but he couldn't land in jail. So he'd just practiced PR spins in case accusations ever attempted to ruin his career. Now they might come in handy to save his ass in a different way.

Time for 'Operation Reformed,' he thought.

"Oh, yes, I do remember you . . . " he said, although her name and face were still just a notch on his mental bedpost. "I'm so sorry. You have every right to be furious with me. Manipulation for sexual intimacy is wrong. My actions back then were wrong. Those were the demons I battled in pursuit of my best self. I'm thankful that I'm no longer that person anymore."

"I don't know if I believe that." Claire tapped the butcher knife against her pursed lips. "If you've learned your lesson, life wouldn't have sent you to me."

"I have a serious girlfriend. Her name is Lindsey. Surely you've seen our pictures together."

"Yes. You look like the *Came-With-the-Frame* couple. Sickeningly cute. I have my own ideas of what purpose she serves."

"Purpose?"

"Like gay men who get married. She's a girlfriend for hire. So no one accuses you of scamming women still. Does the poor girl know what she is? Or does she think she actually means something to you?"

"Claire, please be reasonable. All signs point to me being a changed man. Lindsey and I are very committed."

"Things are rarely as they seem. But you're right. There's only one way to ensure that you're telling the truth." Claire pulled the grey slacks from his thigh and stuck the blade through the fabric. The blade tore through the leg of his pants easily.

Johnny yelped, then held his breath as she cut away his trousers and boxer briefs. Within two minutes his cock and balls were exposed, framed by the remaining shreds of clothing. Johnny was too scared to worry about how pathetic his genitals looked, shriveled with a week's worth of hair growth since his last shave.

"Are you happy now that I'm humiliated? Are we even?"

"This isn't about getting even. I honestly want to help you. But it's gonna be a struggle for both of us. The struggle is important though. Did you know that when a caterpillar is in the cocoon, transforming, there is immense struggle and pain. Before I dropped out of my first and only year at MCC, my bio teacher showed us a time-lapsed video of the chrysalis and the butterfly fighting to get out. The sides of the sack pulsed so violently I could feel the poor butterfly's pain. I wanted to take a tiny blade and put the smallest of slits in the cocoon. Peel it back and help the creature get out of it quicker. But do you know what happens if you do that?"

"Claire, you aren't making any sense."

"Stop saying my name as if you give a shit about me." Claire stabbed the bed just below his exposed genitals.

The mattress tore and Johnny howled, pulling himself as far away from the blade as he could. "I'll stop!"

"Didn't I tell you to calm down. Bad things are attracted to fear."

"Okay, I'm calm." Johnny tensed his body to stop the tremors. "I'm just trying to understand why you're doing this to me."

"I'm trying to explain, but I need you to listen and focus." Claire placed the weapon on the ground. "After you used me and threw me to the curb, it took a long time to get my life together. I researched a lot of spiritual paths and personal development courses. While they're all a bit different, they do have many similarities. One being this idea that energy flows through centers in the body. All metaphysical of course. Like chakras, and how unbalances in chakra energy can really ruin a person's demeanor and actions—"

Like Santa's magic bag, Claire pulled another object out of her apron. With a flick of her thumb, a purple vibrator buzzed to life.

"You don't teach about energy centers in your courses, but I think they're real. I feel changes in my being and actions whenever I meditate on them. Today, we're going to align your chakras so you won't hurt women anymore—even through your subconscious behaviors. I am giving you the gift of true change to thank you. It's what your infinite self wants."

Johnny's charming tongue fell useless. He stared at the crazy bitch, mouth gaping, brain overloaded with trying to figure out what the hell was happening next.

"The root chakra is your foundation," Claire said. "It's tied to your feelings of stability, safety, and your essential needs being met.

I sense this is the point of your first blockage." Claire pointed the vibrating toy at his crotch. "We're gonna open that chakra up a bit."

"This is not how the law of attraction or chakras work!"

"Each of us must go through hell to find our heaven. But I'll try to be as gentle as possible." Claire spat on the toy, rubbing it up and down.

"You're sick."

"Me? I'm not the one who may be lying to thousands of people about who I really am." She took hold of his cock and balls, lifting them.

"I told you I changed!" Johnny clenched his anus and tilted his pelvis into the bed.

"We'll see."

He fought her attempts to insert the vibrator into his ass until she squeezed his balls. His gut exploded in nauseous pain.

"I know this isn't easy," she said, hand gripping his junk firmly. "Changing your negative traits hurts as much as coming off a drug, I'm sure. I never had to kick a substance addiction, but I've heard stories. Rebuilding my self-esteem a little each day seemed like a similar hell. Miserable. Both physically and emotionally."

Unable to stand the pressure any longer, Johnny unclenched his sphincter and Claire released his balls. He did his best not to wriggle as the semi-wet toy was inserted into his rectum. Johnny had taken slender fingers and tongues in his ass before, but this was different. The vibrator working his ass felt like shitting in reverse. It wasn't painful, but it wasn't pleasurable.

"Ass play, or *root chakra work* as I like to call it, can be extremely pleasurable, activating, and healing. Once you feel the safety and security flowing through you, you'll be able to enter into healthier romantic relationships. Not manipulative power plays of sex."

Johnny kept his eyes on the ceiling, praying for it to be over soon. Let her humiliate him. As long as he could get out alive, the real battle would come later.

"Next, the sacral chakra. The seat of all things sexual and creative. Rather than blocked, this chakra is way too open on you." Claire laughed and pulled out an iron contraption that looked like a suit of armor for a penis. "We need to put some restrictions on your passion. No more compulsive sexual behaviors, you predator."

"I'll quit," Johnny whimpered. "You're right, I have no business coaching other people. I'll take down all the videos, remove the books. No more personal development guru. No more teaching—"

"You still don't get it. I don't want you to quit, Johnny." Claire clamped his balls and flaccid member into the male chastity device. "You really do have the chance to help millions of people. Affirmations and positive thinking aren't bullshit."

Claire stepped back to admire the contraception on his genitalia.

Like the vibrator, it didn't hurt, but it wasn't pleasant.

"After I started personal development. I got into eastern philosophies," she continued. "Then I studied the brain and neuroplasticity and evolutionary traits. There is an element of truth behind your teachings—whether you know it or not. In the beginning, a lot of the work is mechanical, feels foolish and untrue, especially positive affirmations like *I'm good enough*, *people respect me*. But when it becomes natural to say those things, that's when the change happens and you grow. I want you to keep preaching and helping motivate others. "

"If you're a true believer, aren't you worried about the karma involved in this?"

"Karma is all about intent. And my intent is pure. Soon, yours will be too." She pointed to his chest. "Have you guessed why the corset helps?"

"My pec chakra is out of whack," he sneered. "You must be fixing its posture."

"Now you're getting it. The corset is the only thing I could think of to keep the solar plexus—the heart chakra—bound, and there was no way I could put it on with you conscious. With this chakra too open, you've probably been obsessing over your vanity in an unhealthy way, and it's a big factor in your dominating and toxic personality rather than the strong supportive personality you could be."

Claire stepped back and appraised him like a piece of art. Johnny looked away, scared of how much more was still to come.

"Say cheese."

He looked back and Claire was walking around him snapping pictures with her cell phone.

"Now the truth comes out. I should have known it was black mail."

"I don't want money." Claire sat on the bed, resting the knife tip on the soft skin where his throat met his chest. "Two years ago, when I first tried manifesting this moment, I visualized opening your throat chakra with this."

She pushed the tip of the knife a bit harder, then pulled it away.

Johnny could feel a pearl of blood drip from the tiny prick. His mind was numb. Words didn't feel like they could save him anymore.

"You never answered my question." She moved the knife to his forehead, just above his nose and between his eyes. "Do you know what happens if you cut into the butterfly's cocoon too early?"

He tried to look away again and the knife scratched him but not deep. Claire grabbed his jaw, forcing him to look into her eyes.

"If you cut the sack too early—even to help—the butterfly that emerges will never fly. They just sit on the tree branch until death. The struggle inside the cocoon actually pumps fluid into their wings, which help the wings expand, strengthen, and develop. My bio teacher explained that if you cut them out early, that entire process of development would be lost. Hence robbing the creature of flight. Had he not told me, I wouldn't have known. I could have done such a thing by accident."

"Claire, think about—"

She pushed the blade into his third eye chakra, same as she'd done with his throat.

"I think you knew exactly what you were doing when you cut my sack. When you cut Julie Aguliar's, Andrea Kozimore's, Michelle Sgn's . . . I found a laundry list of girls when I started looking. I wanted to manifest you, so I could open up this third eye of yours, too. Give you a little speech on speaking your inner truth before stabbing you to death. That was wrong though. When I changed my intention to one of helping you, not vengeance, the universe granted my reality. After all, you really did change my life."

The blade pulled from his head and Johnny could now feel his quickly-cooling piss wet the mattress.

"Yuck." Claire stood from the bed.

"What happens now?" he whimpered.

"The butterfly needs to undergo the struggle in the cocoon to be able to fully realize his potential and beauty. Struggle strengthens humans too. Had you not manipulated and hurt me, kicked me when I was already depressed and down, then I would not have hit rock bottom. I needed that before I could rise." She stood and smiled compassionately. "Hopefully, this little adventure has been enough struggle to induce you to change—assuming you are still that same bartender deep down. If I hear of you manipulating another young girl. Using them as a cum dump. If you breakup with your serious girlfriend without compassion and decency. I release these photos to the world, and the ensuing media storm of *Johnny Troutman - Self Development Guru and Sex Bondage Fan* will be enough struggle to change you."

"No one is going to believe I asked for you to do this."

"Don't be so sure. Some of the picture angles are debatable. A quick adjustment in photoshop, and suddenly, you look like you're enjoying yourself." Claire winked. "What's the problem? Just don't manipulate vulnerable people and situations for sex with lies and these will remain hidden in my phone forever. Deal?"

Johnny looked down at his corset, chastity, belt, and vibrating anus. "I get to leave?"

Claire nodded.

"Deal."

Claire smiled, then bent down and turned off the vibrator. Pulling it from his ass, she placed it to the side and began unclamping his chastity armor.

"Once a little time goes by, the sharp edge of this trauma may blunt. So I suggest S.P.A and Be-Do-Have to help your fortitude. And if you ever get the idea that these pictures aren't so bad . . . " Claire looked at him with those green eyes of fiery intensity. "You are gonna have no defense for the ones I took while you were still unconscious. Trust me. Be good. Be true."

"Wait," he said as she walked to the door. "Untie me."

Claire took a Clorox wipe from the apron and cleaned the knife. She placed it on the bed just out of reach from his tied hand.

"I'm not sure when this cozy cabin is being rented out next. But I'm sure you can manifest your way out before then." She smiled and returned to the door. "Namaste, Johnny."

HELL COMES TO THE BURGER HUT

MATT WEBER

A PORTLY FAMILY of four sits at the front window of the Burger Hut, each of them stuffing their faces. The restaurant staff appears shorthanded—only three workers in sight, and they're all buried in their duties.

These hicks won't know what hit them.

My wife sits alone stationed at a corner table across the lobby, pretending to sip a fountain drink. She gives me a wink. Jet-black hair, deep blue eyes, and a smile to charm a snake. Natalie possesses a beauty that can leave a man speechless. I'm lucky to have her. She's the love of my life and my top operative.

We're stationed off I-65 in a suburban podunk called Trapper Valley, Alabama. I selected this place for its proximity to the freeway, but also because of its disgusting everyday Pax Americana.

Fast-food lovers are treated to cheap, wobbly plastic chairs scattered around eight rickety foldaway tables. Two condiment islands divide the lobby's black-and-white checkered floor from the long cashier's counter. Along the glass-paned front wall squats a row of three dining booths with a captain's view of the interstate on-ramp.

At the table next to us, a skinny boy with a gawky face takes a seat across from a chubby girl with acne. The teenagers hold hands and close their eyes. They bow their heads and mumble something.

Amen, he says.

The kid removes a small carton from a greasy paper sack, places it in front of him and opens the top. The smell of cooked meat clouds the air. He plunges a fork into his chili dog. Visions of slaughterhouses and offal piles rush through my mind. I hear the squealing of pigs and the baying of dying cattle. I see the glassy, terror-filled eyes of the animals, and see their gaping, pleading mouths calling for help that will never come.

The boy lifts up a plug of the frank as a brown lump of spiced beef plops off the fork. He shoves the bite onto his tongue and chews with his mouth open, smacking his food as juice runs downs his chin.

A gray-haired man in a leather jacket walks through the Burger Hut's front door. He greets the woman at the register, "Afternoon, Mabel."

"Howdy, Mayor!" Mabel pushes her bifocals back on her nose and flashes the man a grin.

This is a huge stroke of luck. With a politician in the fold, we can count on a wall-to-wall news blitz. They call that kind of publicity "earned media," and it has more reach than any paid advertisement.

The only other people present are two old biddies having coffee and a loner with a scruffy beard and hunting jacket. He's the type to carry a pistol under that jacket, so I watch him like a hawk.

The time is prime, because the mayor and Mabel are distracted in conversation, and I can tell by Natalie's expression we're on the same page: start with the big fish; don't let him get away.

From her seat, she gives me a glance, one eyebrow raised.

I respond with a nod.

Ready. Steady. Go.

Natalie slips her dark sunglasses on. She rises onto those long, shapely legs and strides across the room in a black mini-skirt and stiletto heels. I noticed Scruffy Hunter eyeballing her earlier, but now when she passes, he looks up from his burger and really drinks her in. It's clear on his face that he knows she "ain't from around here."

I unzip the duffle bag in the chair to my left.

Since the mayor has his back turned, Mabel is the first to notice Natalie. She shifts her eyes from my wife to the mayor and back, unsure how to proceed with the six-foot siren slinking up beside him on the opposite side of the cash register.

Natalie draws up about twelve inches from the mayor, clicks her heels together, and looks at him like he was the Christmas gift she'd always wanted.

When he turns, he actually flinches at the sight of her beauty, his head pulling back, chin tucked in, then he breaks into one of those "vote for me" smiles.

"Why, hellooooo!" he gushes, extending his hand to her. It's obvious from the corny honk of his voice that this guy is a natural panderer. One who loves the ladies.

"Hiiii," she replies in a hiss, short but silken. She should be an actress. "I hear you're the mayor."

She glances back to her corner then adjusts her stance. She wants a more flattering angle for the video camera live-streaming from the tiny tripod where she'd been sitting. Nobody ever got famous for the back of their head.

"That's me." The mayor chuckles. "Guilty as charged." His eyes crawl over Natalie's body, and he can't seem to quit his goofy grin. He looks younger than his gray hair would suggest, and the way he's practically feeding from Natalie's palm tells me he's accustomed to using his position to drop as many panties as he can get away with.

Mabel reappears from nowhere. She slides a paper sack across the counter and tugs on his jacket sleeve. "Your Whammy burger's ready, Mayor."

"Thank you, Mabel." He reaches across his chest and snatches the bag with his left hand without ever dropping his right, which is still awaiting Natalie's handshake. He never takes his eyes off my wife.

The mayor tells her, "I don't believe we've met before."

Natalie touches the red plastic straw of her jumbo fountain drink to the corner of her lips. She stares at him through two black lenses and says, "No, I don't believe we have."

When she takes the mayor's hand, I can tell he's under her spell. I stand up and hook the duffle bag over my shoulder.

"My name is Jimmy Grayson, mayor of Trapper Valley. And I'm sure I haven't seen *you* around town. I've got a knack for faces, and I know I'd remember yours."

"You're right, mayor," she says. "You'd remember me. Because once somebody meets me, they're never the same again."

Natalie releases his hand, peels the lid off her drink, and lays the lid with the straw on the countertop to her left. "My name is The Red Queen, and I'm with the National Humanitarian Front."

He tilts his head and squints but doesn't seem to process what she said. His grin returns. "Well, on behalf of our fine city, I'd like to formally welcome you, and offer one of our famous local delicacies—a Whammy burger! With the works!"

When he extends the paper sack to her, Natalie glares at it with contempt. The mayor has unknowingly flipped a switch, and I can already feel the heat rising in the room.

"I. Don't. Eat. Meat." Each of her words, a drop of acid.

The mayor's smile fades.

Natalie hurls her drink. The liquid inside splashes him right in the face. Mabel gasps while Natalie jumps back to dodge the splatter.

The mayor's head and jacket are soaked, and a new chemical odor joins the smell of sizzling fat. He drops the burger sack and holds his arms out to his sides, looking himself over in disbelief and retreating backward in little steps. He's too distracted to notice me approaching him.

"Why did you . . . " he began. "What did you pour on me?"

Natalie throws her head back and cackles a laugh so cold it gives me a chill. "What did I pour on you?" she says. "Why, it's our secret sauce! So, it's a secret . . . "

She pulls a long-stem barbecue lighter from her rear pocket, and the mayor's angle doesn't let him see the yellow flame click to life behind her back.

God, I love her.

I lift my sawed-off from the duffle bag.

When Ms. Mabel sees me, she tries to warn him. "Mayor, behind you!"

This is helpful, because the mayor turns around to me with his dripping, bewildered face—and away from Natalie, who touches the lighter to his collar.

In a bright flash, he bursts into flames. His scream is worthy of a horror-movie heroine. Everyone in the lobby panics. Everyone except me and Natalie.

I spin on the Scruffy Hunter, who is reaching into his jacket. Is he armed? Having a heart attack? Doesn't matter. I pull the trigger to the sound of thunder. The buckshot blasts him off his chair.

The restaurant workers rush up from the back. Natalie draws the nine from her purse and opens fire. She hits one of them in the chest, and he collapses against a wall. Mabel flees out of sight toward the rear of the building.

The mayor is writhing on the floor and choking on smoke. His clothes turn black like burnt paper. He tries to bat the flames off his face, but his skin sticks to his hands as it melts.

Natalie leaps over the service counter to chase down the workers in the kitchen. I hear the gunshots and know she's got things covered.

The two teens are dashing for the front. I rack the shotgun and fire. A spray pattern rips across the boy's back as he spills out the double doors onto the sidewalk. The girl ahead of him turns back and shouts "Danny!" but at the sight of me and my gun barrel, she keeps running.

A lot of banging and clamor from the kitchen, then I hear a shriek that makes me freeze. Someone stumbles from the kitchen to the front counter, muttering nonsense. The way they slap at the walls, this person must be blind . . . Except, I recognize those flesh-embedded bifocals. It's Mabel, only now she's practically unrecognizable, her face blistered and contorted from screaming and moaning. My wife emerges behind her with a grin, and I realize she must have somehow shoved Mabel down into a fry vat, boiling her in oil.

"Oh, shut up," Natalie says to her. She steps over to Mabel, puts her gun to the woman's temple, and *pow!*

The two elderly women are shuffling toward a side entrance. Natalie vaults over the front counter on a single hand, takes aim and fills their backs with bullets. They fall together in a heap on the floor.

This only leaves the family of fat people frozen in the middle booth.

I step up to their table. The mother is gripping the edge of the table in the throes of some sort of fit. She's hyperventilating, rocking back and forth with her head thrusting to and fro.

The father, in his yellow Hawaiian-print shirt, has his arm around one of his chunky sons. The kid is crying into his dad's chest. The man's other hand is a trembling fist on the table. His face is pasty white, his eyes splayed and watery.

"This is your fault. You realize that, right?" I switch my gaze between each of the parents and tap their trays of half-eaten burgers with the shotgun. "This is what you call food? This is what you teach your children? This is not *food*."

"Please don't hurt us," the father says. "These are my sons Bryan and Keith—"

"Shut up," I tell him. Anything he might say is meaningless. Projecting my voice for the recorded audio, I ask, "What if this meat had been ground from the flesh your sons? Would you call it *food* then? This isn't *food*, it's *violence*. And violence begets violence. We are proof of that."

I rack the gun again. The father tries to stand. He opens his mouth to protest. I shove the barrel between his teeth and squeeze the trigger. The back of his head explodes, painting the window behind him.

I expect more screaming, but they are too shocked to speak. The kid who has bits of his dad speckling his cheek makes a mewling noise and shrinks into the corner.

"Stand up," I order the woman.

"No, no, please no," she whimpers.

Natalie walks up to my side. "Stand the fuck up!"

The woman turns beet-red and mumbles gibberish. She looks like she might liquefy and ooze onto the floor, then Natalie presses a switchblade against her pudgy neck, and the mom goes rigid and shuts the hell up.

"Stand," Natalie tells her.

The mom struggles to her feet.

"Walk."

She slouches ahead as instructed—a drab-looking woman with dishwater hair.

Halfway across the lobby, Natalie orders, "On your knees."

The mom closes her eyes and obeys. They're both facing Natalie's camera.

Standing behind the woman, my wife looks into the lens. "We're from the National Humanitarian Front and we're here to make a statement! For ages, you people have killed the innocent to satiate your gluttonous appetites. Those of us with a sense of empathy have tried to reason with you and persuade you to change your ways. Still, you persist, and we now have no recourse but to take an eye for an eye."

I step next to Natalie, right into what should be the video frame, just like we practiced. I glare straight ahead, rack the shotgun, and shout, "Viva la revolution!"

Then, I aim. The blast spreads the mother's face all over the live-streaming camera lens. This theatrical touch was Natalie's idea, and while I haven't seen it from our viewers' perspective, I bet it looked gnarly.

"This is the new reality," Natalie declares. "Today is a day of change! Those of us who value peace, nature, and equality can no longer sit idly by as the flesh-eaters continue their barbaric exploitation of animals. The time of enlightenment is at hand. We are the N.H.F., and to punish the guilty is the most humane thing we can do in our new society."

I rack the gun and blow the camera to pieces, ending our live feed. This "explosive finale" was another of my wife's ideas.

I turn to Bryan and Keith. The young boys are now little more than shellshocked mounds of jelly. I give Natalie a shrug, then walk toward the car. Time to split.

As I reach the door, I turn around and half-expect to see Natalie stabbing the boys with her knife. Instead, she's jogging to catch up with me, sporting a coy expression as if she knows what I'd been thinking. And she probably does.

She loops her arm around mine, and we push through the double doors together, heading to our car.

Just outside, the crack of gunfire. The door behind us shatters.

"Go!" I shout to Natalie. I rack my last shell, but I've got no idea who's shooting at us or from where. Based on the spray of glass, the shooter is probably to our right. We haul ass to the left. Lucky for us, that's where our ride is parked.

Someone fires twice more, but we make it across the parking lot. Natalie is ahead of me. I slide in loose gravel and fall on my hip. More shots ring out.

Natalie spills forward.

NO!

I scramble to my feet and run to her side. I see blood. *Blood!* I scoop her up. She's not responding. Throwing her arm over my neck,

I hoist her by the ribs, spinning around to see the mystery shooter take aim at us from the far side of a Taurus. It's the chubby girl with acne, Danny's girlfriend, armed with a pistol. I thrust out the twelve-gauge and fire a one-handed shot that only blasts the paint off the top of the Ford. But the girl ducks for cover, and that's what I need. I make a break for it, dragging Natalie with me. We get to the Jeep, and I stuff her into the passenger seat then roll across the hood to the driver's side.

I leap into the vehicle. The keys are waiting. I crank the ignition. Another gunshot, and glass sprinkles onto my lap. I duck down in the seat, throw the gear into reverse and peg the gas. The jeep lurches backward. We bang into another car. I cut the wheel and jam it into drive, peeking out the window to see the teenager realigning her sights. With a stomp on the accelerator, we swerve out of the parking lot, screeching the tires, and bound onto the road headed for the freeway on-ramp.

I hear one more shot, but it goes astray, and now we're speeding hell-for-leather away from the scene of the crime. Natalie is leaning against the car door.

"Sweety? Honey? Can you hear me? You okay?"

She makes a noise. I can't tell what she says, but it's a *noise* dammit! That's *something*!

"Look at me, honey. How bad are you hurt?"

She groans and sighs. She twists toward me and touches her forehead. Her right eye is a red ruin.

"Oh, baby, I'm so sorry."

"My head hurts . . . " she mutters and leans back against the door, closing her one good eye.

I merge onto the interstate and hit power on the radio. I dig through static and top-40s channels until I hit a news broadcast.

"*. . . The shooting in Dallas is the fifth attack reported today across the United States, with similar incidents taking place near Pittsburg, Detroit, Los Angeles and Memphis. Speculation is mounting that these separate events are coordinated attacks tied to domestic terrorism.*"

It's really happening.

I scan for a different channel and hear a local anchor say:

"*. . . Breaking news—we're getting an advance report of some* *sort of mass casualty event at a fast-food restaurant off I-65 near exit 272. That's the Trapper Valley exit. Brenda, what's the latest word on this?"*

Just wait until our video goes viral. It's going to be a hit.

"Mission accomplished, baby!" I tell her. "We are now part of something much bigger than ourselves. They'll be talking about this day for the rest of our lives."

We're zipping down the freeway in pace with traffic, and nobody around seems to have any idea that we're two mass murderers making our escape. Two revolutionaries.

"You gonna be okay, hon?" I ask.

Natalie barely grunts a response, but I know she's exhausted. I should let her rest. A shame about her eye, but we'll get her all fixed up. And one thing's for sure, my wife will look smokin' hot in an eyepatch.

I pop open the center console. I pull out a beef stick and snap into a Slim Jim, picturing a cattle gun pressed to the head of a cow. With a sharp pop, a bolt penetrates the skull. The animal shudders and falls. The meat is so salty, spicy and damned tasty.

Truth is, we don't give a shit about anyone else's cause or agenda. Natalie and I are in it for the glory, and there's a whole lot of people all over the world who will celebrate everything we just did.

THE LONG WINTER AHEAD

THOMAS K.S. WAKE

MAYBE THIS STOP wasn't such a bad idea after all,"
Nick said, looking at the firm ass of the waitress who just
took their order.

Troy nodded. The waitress could not have been older than
twenty-five and her soft, pinkish skin was like an inviting waistband
under her bikini top that cradled her voluptuous chest.

"Sure, wouldn't mind a piece of that." Troy's eyes followed the
swaying buttocks of her jean shorts.

"What about Mary?"

"Well, she's not here, is she?"

"Oh, she is so lucky to have you."

Troy smiled and sipped his beer.

"You got to stick it in where you can while you can before they
entrap you. Trust me, otherwise you die miserable and full of regret.
Or do you disagree?"

Nick shook his head and smiled.

"I kind of like the idea of only one woman for me for the rest of
my life. Waking up next to the same face after a sticky night of
passion."

"Dude, you got to stop watching *Bachelorette*." Troy smiled back.

A local country artist was abusing his guitar on a small stage.
Half a dozen drunken men were swaying on an area which might
have been called a dance floor if one was being generous. From the
thirty or so tables, almost all were full of equally drunk men.

"This place is homey."

"C'mon, don't be a dick." Nick counted only eight women, but they were all young, and even the less attractive ones, were pleasing to his eye. "Just look at the chicks here, and besides, you can't find atmosphere like this in New York."

"Whadda you know? We got ourselves a pair of real-life Yorkers here!"

Nick turned with a snarky comeback loaded, but when he saw the girl who had made the comment, the words shriveled in his throat.

The pint froze on Troy's lips as he stared at two girls. The one who spoke wore a red leather miniskirt, that clung to her skin, drawing out the perfect round shape of her ass. A tattered, white tank-top squeezed her large breasts. Her red hair was in two loose ponytails, cascading down either side of her face, framing the delicate features. Sitting down, she blew a pink bubble of gum.

"That glass glued to your mouth?" She reached over and removed the pint from Troy's hand and took a long, slow sip. When she removed the glass from her lips, a trickle of beer flowed between her breasts, foaming at the little valley formed in between them.

"Oops," she said and wiped her mouth. "I guess I need practice swallowing."

Nick coughed. He was no stranger to gorgeous women, but such directness was something he wasn't used to.

"Tammy, behave," said the other girl and huddled next to Nick. "I am sure these decent boys aren't used to such crass behavior. Am I right, boys?"

Nick got hard from the smell of the girl. It was intoxicating. Her breasts pulled the tight t-shirt from her midriff, revealing smooth white skin. The nipples were two alluring bumps, telling Nick she didn't wear a bra. Her brown hair was short and gelled up in spikes. Nick liked it and wanted to have her. But the girls looked young. Maybe too young, so Nick tried to pour mental ice on his balls and act cool.

"No. I've been around plenty of crass girls," Troy stammered.

Nick buried his face in his hands.

"Jesus Christ, man."

"Wait, I mean—"

"Stop talking," Nick said.

Both girls laughed, and the sound was like wind-chimes in a light breeze.

"We're just messing with you. This loose lip is Tammy, and I'm Charlene."

Tammy popped another bubble as the guys introduced themselves.

"My lips are the only thing that's loose. So, what brings you two strapping young lads to our neck of the woods?"

"We're heading to our friend's bachelor party and needed a pit stop before driving all the way to Las Vegas."

"Stiff drinks and some local gals, eh?" Tammy casually put her hand on Troy's thigh, but it still sent tingling waves up to his crotch.

"I for one, am glad you did." Charlene looked at Nick, mouth arched in an alluring smile.

"Aren't you girls a bit too young to hang out in a bar?"

Troy looked at Nick with daggers.

Charlene threw her head back and laughed.

"Don't worry boys, we ain't jail-baiting you. We're older than we look."

Tammy popped a bubble and tilted her head like a dog who was listening.

The waitress brought the orders. She placed a greasy burger sitting on a bed of fries in front of Troy and a plate of brown hash for Nick.

He noticed grooves on the woman's face he hadn't noticed earlier. She didn't look as young as he'd first thought, but still stunning.

"Here you go. I see you've found some spring chickens to go with your beer."

The color vanished from Nick's face. Fuck, the girls were under aged.

"Ma'am, I swear we didn't do any—"

The waitress laughed. She winked at Tammy and Charlene.

Nick and Troy were baffled.

Tammy took a ketchup-laced fry from Troy's plate and sucked it clean. She folded the fry in half and pulled it to her mouth using her tongue.

"Mom is just messing with you."

Nick almost choked on his beer.

"Mom? Whose? Yours?"

The waitress curtsied.

"A beer, please," Tammy said.

"Sure, love. And for you, Char?"

"A tequila sunrise, please."

Charlene took Nick's burger and chomped a bite out of it.

"So, where were we?" she said with a mouth full of beef.

"I hope you guys don't have an early departure tomorrow," Tammy said and took another swig from Nick's pint.

On the stage, the musician started a new song. The melody was solemn, and made Nick think of a dark, deep Louisiana swamp.

The singer began to caw the lyrics, and Troy smiled at the out-of-key singing.

"He sure has an . . . interesting style."

"You mean Keith? He's a magnificent guitarist but can't sing for shit."

The waitress brought the drinks and just nodded when Nick asked for a refill.

"So, what do you do when you're not hanging out in bars, alluring strangers to buy you drinks?"

Charlene put her hand on her chest in an overdramatic motion and gasped in fake offense.

"What are you implying, my dear sir?"

"There is no way either of you are twenty-one."

"We have good genes here. The clean rural air and all."

Nick smiled. He doubted the waitress was their mom, but even if it was all a ruse, he didn't mind buying a pretty girl a beer.

"I teach fifth grade and Tammy here is a cantor of sorts," Charlene said.

"What? Seriously?"

Tammy smirked and jiggled her eyebrows.

"Why? Is that hard to believe?"

"You are way too hot to be a cantor. Or any church person." Disappointment crept across Troy's face.

"Oh, don't worry. I'm off the clock." She slid her hand up Troy's thigh and squeezed his balls so hard he winced. "But I have a pretty strong feeling, that I might be calling out to God tonight."

"You are something."

"You have no idea." Tammy fished Troy's earlobe into her mouth and sucked it.

Charlene whispered something to Nick that made him smile.

"Sure. Why not?" Nick answered.

"Sure what?" Troy asked, while Tammy slid her tongue into his ear.

The drive was about a half an hour from the bar. Nick made the judgment call to take his car instead of a taxi, even though he felt the beer was going to his head. Charlene's suggestion to retreat somewhere *more private* followed by a tight pinch of his nipple had made him want to expedite the journey. Plus, it would allow them to leave at first light.

The large two-story log house stood at the end of a long driveway with pines on both sides of the road, which opened to an expansive yard that was cuddled by a heavy forest expanding to what seemed like infinity. A secluded and a beautiful place.

"Whose house is this?"

"My family's," Charlene answered. "Don't worry. Nobody's home. And we have plenty of room, so we don't have to listen to those two."

Troy and Tammy were at it like teenagers. She pressed Troy against the car the minute they got out and injected her tongue back where it had been most of the trip, in his mouth.

"C'mon."

The moment they stepped inside, Tammy pulled Troy into one of the dark hallways.

"See ya!" she hollered, and the darkness swallowed the pair.

"You seem to do this a lot."

Charlene ran her finger along Nick's chest, slipped it into his jeans and pulled him close. Her sweet, almost syrupy smell assaulted his sinuses and made his head sway.

"Does it bother you?" She licked his lips.

"Not really." He grabbed Charlene by the waist and pulled her in. Her breasts pushed against him, perky and firm. Nick's groin responded and swelled.

Charlene led him up the stairs and pushed him onto a bed in one of the rooms. Nick tried to pull her on top of him, but she slammed him back down harder than it seemed possible for a woman that size. She lowered herself and unbuttoned his pants. Nick's penis pushed for freedom against his Calvin Klein's.

Charlene kissed the bulge. Nick held his breath, biting his lip. Charlene pulled the underwear down and released the prisoner. It uncoiled like a meaty spring and slapped Charlene's chin.

"Sorry."

Charlene just smiled and twirled her tongue around the base of his shaft. Nick's penis was throbbing, almost unable to take the blood flowing into his corpus cavernosum. His glans had turned bright purple. Charlene licked the entire length of his penis, and when she reached the tip, she opened her mouth and swallowed him whole. Her mouth was warm and welcoming.

Nick tensed as Charlene pushed him deeper down her throat, her tongue sliding from side to side along the shaft.

Nick was ready to cum when Charlene pulled his penis out of her mouth with a hard *pop*. She got on top of him and sat on his cock.

Charlene kissed him and Nick tasted his pre-cum on her lips. He panted under Charlene's grinding buttocks, losing control to pure lust.

A sudden crash from downstairs made Nick snap off from Charlene's lip lock.

"What was that?"

"Probably Tammy looking for drinks. Sounds like Troy already blew his load." Charlene pressed against Nick's mouth again.

Another crash followed by a heavy *thump.*

Nick forced Charlene off him and tucked his rock-hard manhood into his underwear.

"There's someone in the house." He got off the bed.

"Maybe they're just doing it rough. Come back," she begged.

"Hush."

Nick pressed his ear against the door. Heavy footsteps were coming up the stairs. Heavier than Tammy or Troy could have made. Nick backed away from the door.

"What is it?" Charlene asked.

"There is someone in the hallway outside and it is not Tammy or Troy."

Charlene joined him at the door.

"Don't!"

She disregarded Nick and pulled open the door. There was a deep darkness outside, but nothing more. Charlene poked her head out.

"Tammy? Troy?" She turned to Nick. "See? There's no one there."

Nick peered into the darkness. The moment his head was past the door jamb, a massive hand grabbed him by the neck and pulled him into the hallway, hoisting him off his feet. He weighed a pound over two hundred, but the assailant was holding him in the air with one hand. Fingers like thick dried sausages wrapped around his neck, fingertips reaching his windpipe and cutting off the flow of air. Nick began to gag. He grabbed the fingers and tried to pry them off, but they were welded into his skin.

"Bob!"

The giant eased up a bit. Nick wheezed.

"You do not harm the seed. How many times do I have to tell you?!"

The man holding Nick grunted like a dog that was being reprimanded by his master.

Nick tried to speak.

Charlene ignored him.

"I swear to Grandma, that if you hurt the other one, you are so going to get it!"

The grip loosened and Nick collapsed on the floor. His oxygen deprived brain was unable to force his feet to move.

The man who had grabbed him was massive, blocking the entire hallway, his shoulders brushing the walls and the top of the head touching the ceiling. In the dark, it was impossible to make out any details, but his head was misshapen, like a Jack O' Lantern that had rotted and collapsed.

"Who . . . ? What . . . ?"

"Nick, this is my brother Bob. Bob, this is Nick."

Bob bent down and picked up Nick. When he brought his face closer, Nick gasped.

Bob's face looked like a huge deformed chaga mushroom that had been bound with strips of birch bark, like a mummy. Black peat-like stuff was bulging from between the strips. The hulk smelled like mulch.

"What the fuck?"

A black slit appeared where a normal person would have a mouth. Bob was smiling. He bent down and punched Nick in the face, sending him into unconsciousness.

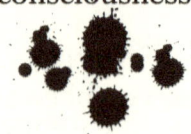

Nick was dangling when his mind crept back into him. Something thick was pressing against his stomach. It was Bob's arm curled around his waist, carrying him like a sack of potatoes. A gentle wind was blowing, and Nick's legs felt chilly. He only had his underwear on.

Bob's skin smelled sweet, like it was slathered with honey and pear that had started to ferment. Nick looked to his right and saw something poking from Bob's other hand. It was someone's foot. Troy.

Something kept caressing his back and bare feet. Branches. They were in the forest.

"Troy . . ."

"Welcome back, sunshine." It was Charlene. Nick could hear a faint pop behind him. Tammy and her chewing gum.

"Troy is still sleeping. Bob has a tendency to use excessive force on the seed."

"Didn't mean to," Bob said, stopping.

"It's okay, sweetie," Charlene said and patted Bob's cheek.

"What's happening?" Nick stammered.

Charlene's face appeared next to him. In the scarce moonlight siphoning through the canopy of branches and leaves, Charlene looked different. Her face had lost its youthfulness. She had big bags under her eyes and her cheeks were drooping.

"We're going to introduce you and Troy to the rest of the family. C'mon, Bob. Grandma and the rest are waiting."

Nick registered an orange glow intensifying as they continued walking deeper into the woods. The color was restless, jumping from tree to tree, creating frantic shadows that swirled and weaved around them. He lifted his head and saw a huge bonfire flickering in the distance.

They emerged from the thicket into a clearing and Bob put his cargo down.

A large mound with a narrow opening protruded from the ground behind the bonfire. Around the fire, Nick saw people. As the haze dissipated from his head, Nick recognized some of the faces from the bar, but all their appearances had aged.

"What the fuck is going on?"

Nick stood up, trying to figure out a means to escape. He had no idea how fast Bob was, but even if he ran for it, he couldn't leave Troy behind. In the glow of the bonfire, he saw the giant clearly for the first time. Bob was almost eight feet tall. His tree trunk arms were covered in thick, dark hair that looked like moss hanging from the bib overalls.

"You have been chosen to receive a high honor," a raspy female voice announced from behind the flames. It was the sound of air through a punctured lung.

A frail figure leaning on a forked branch approached them. Deep grooves ran across her face and her dark brown skin hung loose. Two emaciated legs poked out from a pair of jean shorts that barely stayed on her skeletal hips. Saggy breasts peeked out from under a bikini top like two chili peppers left out in the sun for too long. She must have been at least ninety years old.

The elderly woman wobbled over to Troy. She sighed deep.

"Bob?" she said with what could almost be affection in her voice. "Take the body and bring it to the saplings."

Bob grunted. As he moved toward Troy, Nick bolted. Tammy seemed to have expected that and punched Nick in the chest with a force that cracked his sternum. A jolt of pain shot through his torso and the air was knocked out of him. He collapsed, wheezing like a marionette whose strings had been severed.

Tammy knelt to pick him up. Her youthful features were a perversion of what they had been, the skin was hanging from her face as if the skull underneath had shrunk and the lively pink of her exposed belly was now cadaver grey.

Charlene stepped next to Tammy and was changing as she moved. Her face was that of a wax figure set too close to a heat source and was now sliding off.

"What the hell are you people?"

Nick crawled backward toward the bonfire. Behind the two grotesque creatures, more people emerged into the clearing from the shade of the woods.

Nick was surrounded.

He let out a squeal when Bob took hold of him. He was like a baby in the massive hand and resisting the towering behemoth was impossible. With the other hand, Bob took Troy by the neck, dragging him like a cat hauling around her kittens.

Nick felt a lump in his throat. If he hadn't wanted to stop and rest, they'd soon be arriving in Vegas, getting ready to join the gang who had started to drink at noon the previous day. He had no delusions how this was going to end and started sobbing.

"Jesus Christ. Get it together," Charlene said, still melting.

"I don't want to die."

Both Charlene and Tammy let out a caw that might have been a laugh.

"Why on earth would we kill you?"

Nick was confused. He snorted in the snot running down his upper lip.

"What are you going to do with me?"

"We are going to take you to see our grandmother."

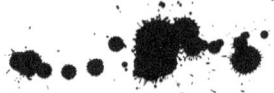

There was a thick, cloying smell hovering inside the mound. Bob's shovel-sized palm on his shoulder pushed Nick through the tunnel. Bob's frame scraped the sides of the narrow passage. Thin roots hung from the earthen ceiling, snaking down the walls like irregular chicken mesh. In front of Nick walked the old woman and four men carrying torches. There was a steady murmur coming from behind them as the rest of the people poured into the mound.

Ahead of the old woman, was the glow of light. More fire.

The tunnel opened into a cave about 150 feet in diameter and little less in height. Scattered along the walls were large brazen cauldrons, fire crackling inside them. On the opposite side of the doorway stood a tall tree that looked like an oak. Its dead branches touched the cave ceiling and spread across it, coming down the walls, like it was supporting the mound.

Something stirred behind the tree. Round, tubular shapes impossible to count, turning, twisting, lashing out and slithering around each other.

Bob gave a sharp push, knocking Nick off his feet. He proceeded to throw Troy's body on the writhing mass. The shapes wormed over Troy, wrapping around his lifeless body. Bulbous growths pushed from their long bodies, opening to reveal a maw of chaotic thorns. Nick had to turn away as the growths began to nibble and suckle on Troy's stiffing body.

The people gathered in the chamber began to chant in a low, steady rhythm that rose and fell, rose and fell.

The tree responded to the choir. Its branches shivered, the trunk shifted, and it seemed to grow like a flower straightening its stem toward the sun after a dark night. The rugged bark was re-organizing itself, sliding and turning.

The old woman lifted her arms toward the treetop and began to speak with devotion. Nick didn't understand the language, but he was mesmerized. The words acted like water to a dying flower; the shiver in the branches quickened and the tree soughed.

The circle of people tightened, closing in on the tree. Pairs of hands grabbed Nick's armpits and yanked him up. His legs refused to carry him. Nick recognized Keith holding him on his left side. He, too, looked at least thirty years older than a few hours ago on stage, but still his grip was so strong that Nick feared it might crush his arm.

The old woman turned, and her gaze locked with Nick's.

"I want you to know that we are eternally grateful to you for your contribution."

"What fucking contribution?"

The old woman smiled and stepped away, making room for Nick to be carried to the tree. The face of a woman was in the trunk. The features weren't carved in, but almost like the ancient woman was pushing through the bark from inside.

"I don't want to die."

The old woman laughed.

"My dear son. This is not about death; this is about life."

She motioned to Charlene, and the woman got on her knees and pulled down Nick's underwear. The shifting of the bark intensified, and the branches shook, anticipating something.

"What the fuck are you doing?"

Charlene fished Nick's flaccid penis between her wrinkly lips with her tongue.

"Get off me!" Nick struggled, but the grip of the two men held. Charlene's hand was like sandpaper as she massaged Nick's balls to the rhythm of her sucking. There was nothing arousing in Charlene's appearance, but her mouth was warm and wet. Her tongue found its way under his foreskin, and she licked around the glans. Despite his resistance, Nick was getting hard.

"Good boy."

Charlene pulled his penis out with a *smack*, thick saliva running from her mouth. She ran her tongue over his testicles, along the shaft, and then took the entire member inside, gagging until he was hard as marble.

Nick whimpered as Charlene worked him harder, faster, and wetter.

Suddenly, she stopped.

"He is ready."

She stepped aside and Nick saw that the face in the trunk had opened its eyes and was smiling. The branches were curved toward him, the skeletal ends waggling like the legs of an upturned centipede.

About four feet under the face, the bark had subsided and revealed a vertical slit, with plump, round edges. Viscous brown sweet-smelling liquid was dripping from the hole.

The eyes of the carved face widened, and its mouth opened in a sigh of anticipation.

Keith and the other guy dragged Nick toward the tree. The closer they got, the more fervent the tree became. Its leaves and branches shook and the liquid seeping from the slit was bubbling like spittle on the lips of a passed-out drunk.

The trio stopped a foot from the tree. The old woman spoke, half vocalizing, half speaking:

"The Mother of Gaia. Grandmother of us all. Take this gift and bless us with Yours."

The crowd gathered around, still chanting. The old woman continued:

"You who have always been here and Who will always be. Bless us!"

"Bless us!" begged the crowd.

Charlene reached around and grabbed Nick's penis. Her hand was wet with spit and she started to pump, keeping Nick ready, sliding his foreskin back and forth over the tip with her thumb and forefinger.

"Please stop."

She didn't. The men holding Nick pushed him forward and Charlene guided the erected penis inside the slit.

"Fuck her!" the crowd chanted.

"No!"

The men pulled Nick's arms over and around the tree, pushing his face against the carved one.

"Fuck her!"

Nick didn't move. He was afraid his shoulders would pop out of the sockets.

The mouth of the carved face opened, and a rugged splint came out and started licking Nick's cheek.

"Fuck her! Fuck her!"

The crowd chanted faster and faster.

Nick held his ground. He tried to will his penis down, but the insides of the tree were warm. The liquid oozing on his groin sent tingles through his entire body.

"Suit yourself," Charlene whispered, her voice like gravel tumbling down a drainpipe.

She took a hold of Nick's pelvis and started lifting it up and pushing it down. Up and down. Up and down.

"Fuck her!"

The splint lathered on Nick's face, the thin insect leg-like branches caressed his neck and slithered under his shirt. His lower belly made a sloshing sound as it hit the tree just above the slit. The brown liquid splashed around them. The tree was getting wet as Nick was forced to make love to it.

Charlene cackled.

Nick felt the climax building in his abdomen. The want to ejaculate grew stronger.

Charlene sensed it and she hastened his thrusting.

The splint found its way inside Nick's mouth the moment he came. His muscles spasmed and his testicles pumped the semen inside the living tree. Charlene released her hold, took Nick's testicles, and milked them to get every last drop.

The tree was shaking, its branches shot upward and spread like a broken umbrella.

The crowd clapped! The chant changed.

"Nick! Nick! Nick!"

Nick was released and he slumped to the ground, his torso covered in thick brown liquid. It smelled sweet. Like sap.

He stared at the ceiling and the expanding branches of the thing, and still he had a hard time believing it actually existed.

The thin branches pulsated. Something was moving inside them, starting from the tree, and making their way to the tips. They were growing thicker. Bright flowers blossomed on every branch, making the ceiling look like a kaleidoscope of colors.

The carved face was smiling with its mouth open, the splint tongue flapping at Nick like a serpent.

The stamens burst open and ejected what looked like wet pinecones suspended from a stalk.

Everyone in the chamber looked up, extending their arms to reach for the cones.

The branches bent down, and hungry hands grabbed the harvest of the tree.

Nick saw Keith sinking his teeth into a cone. It was soft and sinuous, black veins zigzagging on the surface like tiny rivers of ink. It popped when Keith's teeth punctured the chewy, fleshy skin. Brown mucous dripped from his mouth onto his chin, but Keith gathered everything up with his fingers and licked them clean.

Nick felt pressure in his head as his sanity was about to leave him. Everyone in the crowd was feasting on a fleshy pinecone, licking the content from their fingers and off of each other. Sickly pops sounded like the crackling of muted firecrackers as everyone went for more.

Nick glanced over to Charlene. Her face was tightening. The color seeped back into her hair and the boobs that had been sagging, swelled like balloons. The floppy skin under her arms retracted, and the shade of liver melted away, revealing pink, youthful skin.

All around Nick, the people who had just moments ago seemed like a group of pensioners, regained their looks and vigor. Tammy was again a stunning redhead.

Not five minutes had passed, and the chamber was filled with people who seemed to be in their prime.

A woman with jean shorts and a bikini top bent over Nick. It was the waitress, restored to her youthful, perky appearance.

"What are you?"

Charlene laughed and the rejuvenated crowd gathered around him, but no one answered.

"We are all in your debt. We haven't had such a strong *Plucking* in decades. You are a spunky young man. Thank you."

A wave of agreement washed over the crowd.

Hope sparked inside Nick.

"So, you're going to let me go?"

The waitress laughed.

"Go? Don't be silly."

She waved and two men grabbed Nick, hoisting him up. Charlene, young and desirable came and knelt, caressing Nick's buttocks.

"We have to make it through the winter and our storages are empty," she said, wrapping her tender, warm lips around Nick's penis and starting to suck again.

The slit in the tree began to ooze.

GENITAL GORGONZOLA

MONTAGUE WHITE

AS I GAZE into my wife's excited eyes across the dinner table, with the naked, filthy, reeking, quivering man laid out between us, our spoons poised over his rotting and partially liquefied penis, I tell myself, "This is how to keep the magic alive."

She leans toward me for a kiss, pressing her spoon into the crumbly, creamy matter protruding from the cracked foreskin as she does so.

"Careful," I say . . . but too late. One of the many maggots writhing in the subtly souffléd organ beneath us hurls itself upward, artfully finding its way between her slightly parted lips like a particularly well aimed shot of cum. She giggles with delight and smiles, showing me the maggot now wriggling feverishly on her tongue. She continues to lean in, thrusting her tongue at me and I close my mouth around it hungrily, relishing the feeling of the maggot's agitated contortions and delightedly discovering hints of the spicy sensation we are about to consume.

"I love you," I sigh.

"Let's eat!" she replies.

Time to tuck in. This may just be the greatest delicacy in the world, the human version of *Casu Marzu*, the Sardinian maggot cheese. Miraculous and highly criminal biology has allowed my subject's genitalia to be receptive to the introduction of the cheese fly. In specially engineered conditions, these flies have done their work, burrowing into flesh and tissue and laying hundreds of eggs. From these eggs, hungry larvae emerged, thriving at first on carefully cultivated smegma before eating their way through root, shaft, glans, skin and testicles. All of which has been suitably digested and excreted by the industriously insatiable larvae to produce our dish. Genital Gorgonzola! *Cojones Camembert!*

I'm drooling. I can hear the man's feeble moans as we dip into the phallic fondue. The taste of the cock curd is all the more piquant for his panic and pain. There will of course be fresh perspiration, a perfect complement. I lift the weak arm nearest to me and thrust my nose and lips into the richly rank armpit, inhaling the odor of his anguish and lapping greedily at the sweat drenched hairs.

This brings my subject to the climactic point we've been anticipating. A bubbling surge of watery feces bursts out of him. I plunge my head between his legs, licking this exquisite chutney from the underside of his thighs. I push both arms under him and heave him upwards so that I can reach his raw, weeping anus and suck directly from the source.

Almost drunk with delight I step back to let my wife take her fill. Watching her head nuzzling the sopping and soiled remains of our subject's maggot-ridden manhood I am aware that I have never felt a deeper love for her than at this very moment. I reach my hand under her chin and lift her radiant, shit-smeared face so that I can once again gaze into her eyes.

"Happy Anniversary, darling."

JEZEBEL

W.R. MACUMBER

JEZEBEL STITCHED HER throbbing wound, thinking about all the times she sewed the rips in Samantha. The doll's cheap fabric would tear open at the seams and white clouds of fluff would spill out. She'd stuff the fluff back inside and mend her with the needle and thread.

In those days, Jezebel's skin was a blank canvas, untouched. Mother said she could have been a model if she had better cheekbones. Other girls envied her because the boys gawked and flirted. She had trouble making friends and spent most of her time reading or drawing.

Then one day, nature turned its back on her. She blossomed early, and like starving dogs, the boys started sniffing around.

Jezebel winced as she tied the last stitch. An autumn chill whistled through gaps in the walls, snuffing out several candles. The smoke drifted toward the ceiling like lost spirits seeking out the promise of heaven. She sat in the gloom, watching the flame of the last candle dance across the cabin's interior.

The cruel kisses from blades and cigarette burns tattooed her stomach and thighs. Jezebel quickly learned not to fight back and endure the pain. She first ran away after getting her cherry popped, the memory of the man's fat body and cheap cologne forever seared into her mind. She slipped out her bedroom window with only the clothes on her back and a few dollars in her pocket. Mother caught her on the highway, luring her into the car with a smile and empty promises. Those sweet words turned to fists the minute they walked through the door. The beating lasted an hour and the bruises lasted a few weeks, but she learned her place.

For the time being.

Outside, thunder rolled across the valley and rain hissed through the pines. Jezebel wrapped her wound in gauze, wondering if whoever owned the cabin might soon return. Judging by the thickness of dust and abundance of cobwebs, no one had been to the cabin in awhile. There was no food or anything of value inside, but she found a first aid kit and a rusted toolbox.

A small, crippled part of her wanted to die. The peace death would bring whispered in her ears, sweet and tender, except Jezebel wasn't ready. She had been beaten and degraded, but a fire still burned inside of her. She used to confuse the fire for hope, the resilience of the human spirit. Only those were the optimistic desires of a happy, healthy mind. The fire that burned inside of her was sustained by hatred. She wanted to hurt. To cut. To ravage all those who ever defiled and humiliated her.

Mother.

The name gnawed on her mind like a cancerous rat. The town's matriarch had eyes and ears everywhere. Nothing moved without Mother giving her blessing. The whole municipality rested in the palm of her hand, forced into silence by threats or the fistfuls of cash she shoved in their mouths. They were all fat bellied pigs lining up to her trough.

The cabin creaked and groaned in response to the building storm. Her wounds itched, a reminder that they would eventually find her. After years of biding her time, years of calculating every last detail, years of lulling Mother into a false sense of security by feigning defeat and servitude, Jezebel saw an opening and fled.

But Mother hated loose ends and that's exactly what Jezebel was. She survived, for the moment, on borrowed time. Finding an old hunting cabin in the woods had been nothing short of dumb luck, but they would be coming, scouring every highway, back road, trail, and hollow in the Black Pine Hills. And when they caught her, there would be no second chances, no do-over or punishments to endure. Mother would make an example out of her like she did with all the others stupid enough to provoke her hand.

Jezebel opened the toolbox and sifted through the contents.

There was a hammer, a few screwdrivers, a utility knife, loose screws and nails, and a crescent wrench. The tools were rusted and covered in dust.

Over the years she made a habit of drifting deep into the velvet chasms of fantasy. Nothing hurt in these places. In these places, Mother brought her breakfast in bed and hummed while brushing her hair. In these places, the state police kicked in the door, armed with guns and dogs. In these places, Jezebel tackled Mother to the ground, gouging out her eyes and smashing her face until her skull cracked open and gray matter spilled out.

Jezebel gripped the hammer, her knuckles turning white. There was nowhere to run and nowhere to hide. She considered slitting her wrists and dying on her own terms, one last *fuck you* to Mother, but couldn't bring herself to go through with the deed.

Mother had to pay.

The young, naive, and desperate always found their way into Mother's clutches. She preyed on those who fell through the cracks, the lost, and the easily forgotten.

Mother had to pay.

Others would stumble into Mother's web and nobody would do anything because nobody cared. An endless accumulation of desiccated girls, tortured and abused until they were hollow husks of their former selves.

Mother had to pay.

Jezebel placed the hammer back into the toolbox and fastened the clasp. She blew out the last candle, enveloping the cabin in inky darkness. She lay on the floor and stared into the future, preparing for the oncoming storm.

She watched and waited.

Officer Ackerman stopped by the farm at breakfast. He waddled as far as the front porch before Mother came storming out the door, her face contorted in a mask of rage. She gestured wildly, and despite the distance, Jezebel could faintly hear Mother's indignant screeching.

The day continued in the same manner. More and more people

came to the house, all of them bootlickers looking to get into Mother's good graces. Jezebel thought about the black and white westerns she sometimes watched and remembered how the bad guys were wanted *dead or alive*. She wondered how much her head was worth to Mother and then, absently, wondered if Mother was capable of killing or would she get someone to do her dirty work?

At dusk, the farm no longer buzzed with activity. The see-saw chorus of crickets drifted from the cool grass. A gentle breeze caressed the wind chimes on the front porch, the tinkle of bells serenading the setting sun. Jezebel headed for the house using the derelict farm machinery on the edge of the field as cover. The toolbox felt natural in her hands, balanced. She concealed herself behind the old tractor and opened the box. The tools looked hostile in the fading light, as if they were physical extensions of the ugly ideas swirling in Jezebel's head. She held them, enjoying the weight and how they stabilized her shaking hands.

When the sun disappeared beyond the pines, bringing darkness, Jezebel found her way inside the house. She crept through the back porch, opening the door just enough so the hinges wouldn't squeak, and slipped into the kitchen. Jezebel stepped lightly, knowing exactly where to place her feet to avoid the creaks on the floor. She peeked around the corner and saw Jasper sitting in his recliner, watching a baseball game.

Jezebel placed the toolbox on the floor and grabbed the hammer. She eased forward, bent at the waist, so her reflection wouldn't be seen on the television screen. Jasper cleared his throat and shifted in his recliner, scratching the back of his bald head. Jezebel raised the hammer, but hesitated. Jasper stood six-foot four and weighed three hundred pounds, a menacing man to look upon, but he never so much as touched a hair on her head. He always brought Jezebel candy, the good kind, sour watermelon and gummy worms. She let the hammer sag but refused to weaken. Jasper knew what Mother did and went along like an obedient lap dog. His willful ignorance made him guilty and for that he had to pay.

She swung the hammer hard and winced when it made contact. A large gash burst open, exposing bone, but it took a moment for the blood to flow. Jasper jumped to his feet with surprising fluidity for a man his size. He spun around, waving his arms for balance, his eyes wide and confused.

Jezebel swung again, striking him in the face. Several broken teeth skittered across the floor and blood oozed from his split lips. Jasper collapsed to one knee, weakly raising his hands in defense. He tried to say something, but his words came out in a wet stutter.

She swung again and again, striking him over and over. He grunted and groaned with every knock, his arms defending uselessly. Her muscles began to fatigue, but she kept swinging until Jasper toppled over.

His hands trembled and his breathing was fast and shallow. He muttered something intelligible, his blue eyes heavy with betrayal.

She didn't like how he stared at her. She didn't like the emotions his eyes unearthed. She felt vulnerable and exposed.

Jezebel knelt beside him and plunged the hammer into his socket, but the tool wasn't designed to gouge out a pair of eyes. She grunted with exertion, sweat beading on her forehead, and thrust the clawed end as deep as it would go. A wet sucking sound accompanied the grinding of metal on bone. Blood seeped from the mangled socket and the eye squeezed out, still attached to the optical nerve. She repeated the process on the other side, working frantically to relieve herself of the accusing eyes.

The room spun in slow circles and her stomach roiled. Jezebel wobbled from the body and vomited. She hadn't eaten since yesterday's supper, so only a sour and acidic bile splattered to the floor.

The hinges squeaked and the door slammed shut. Heavy footfalls moved across the kitchen and someone opened the fridge.

"No luck yet, but we got a lead," a voice called out. "Has Mother gone to bed?"

Boone!

Jezebel shuddered at the voice and darted across the living room, slipping a flathead screwdriver from the toolbox. She pressed herself against the wall and waited.

Boone wasn't family. He was a mongrel, a pathetic rescue that Mother brought into the house years ago. Everybody loved him and showered him with praise, but Jezebel saw through his sweet manners and gentle smile. He manipulated and exploited others, hiding his true intentions. Boone humiliated and diminished her, but she was through bending to his will.

"Albert Sweetman said someone broke into his hunting cabin last night," Boone said from the kitchen. "Too dark to search the woods, so we decided to start again at first light."

Jezebel readied the screwdriver, licking her lips with anticipation of what needed to be done.

"Jasper? Did you hear a word I said?"

The can of beer slipped from his hand when he saw the mutilated body sprawled on the living room floor. His dull brown eyes were wide and his mouth frozen in an O shape. Jezebel relished the stupid look on his face.

She puckered her lips, whistling a soft, sing-song warble. Boone turned and looked at her, his skin pale and tight.

Jezebel rushed forward and stabbed him in the neck. She gasped, startled by a spurt of something warm and wet striking her face. Boone's blood dripped down her nose, rolling across her lips and coating her tongue. She watched him stumble down the hallway, desperately trying to stop the flow from his artery.

Jezebel stabbed him again, but the screwdriver skipped across his head and ripped a furrow in his scalp. He scrambled, but the blood continued to gush from his neck, turning the floor into a crimson ice rink. His boots found no traction and continuously slid out from under him.

A wet gurgle accompanied Boone's panicked movements. The sight of him slipping and sliding in his own blood was a delightful piece of slap-stick comedy. A tight smile formed on Jezebel's lips. His arrogance and false compassion spilled from his veins. In the throes of death, she saw him for exactly what he was: a scheming bastard who perched on Mother's shoulder and whispered infectious ideas.

"Y-you b-b-bitch . . . " Boone choked on his last words.

Jezebel leaned in close. "I waited a long time for this."

She jammed the screwdriver into his ear and fell forward with all her weight, ramming the tool to the hilt. A strange mewling came from Boone's mouth and grew in pitch. The animal sound sent a shiver down her spine. She winced, unable to understand why he couldn't simply die like the stuck pig he was. Jezebel yanked the screwdriver from his ear and plunged it into his chest. She stabbed and stabbed until the horrible sound ceased.

"What the hell is all the racket about?"

Jezebel stiffened at the grating voice. Mother lingered at the top of the stairs, flicking the light switch on and off to get someone's attention. Jezebel collected the tools and placed them back inside the box. She rounded the corner and stopped at the bottom of the stairs, tucking her hair behind her ear.

Mother took an angry step forward but stopped when she noticed the blood. She gasped and covered her mouth. "Sweet lord in heaven. What have you done, girl?"

Jezebel smiled and began to climb the steps.

"You're sick, baby. Don't you see that? These thoughts and ideas in your head aren't real. Remember what Dr. Cassidy told you?"

"Dr. Cassidy never wanted to help me," Jezebel said. She sat the toolbox down and pulled out the utility knife, extending the rusty blade. "Once I stopped taking all those stupid pills he gave me, I understood the truth."

"You're sick," Mother shouted. "These are fantasies."

Jezebel sneered and lifted the front of her shirt, revealing the cuts and burns. "Is this your idea of fantasy?"

Mother backed away, her eyes never leaving her daughters. "Please, Samantha. I would never do anything to hurt you. You know that, don't you, baby?"

"How many times do I have to tell you? My name isn't Samantha. It's Jezebel!"

She rushed forward, slashing the utility knife in wide arcs. Rather than back away, Mother stepped into her, attempting to isolate the hand holding the knife, but she was too slow. Jezebel slashed Mother across the mouth, slitting a wide gash across her lips.

Mother shrieked and lunged at Jezebel, clawing at her eyes. Jezebel stumbled and fell hard at the edge of the stairs, the air rushing from her lungs.

"You stupid little bitch! I'm going to make sure you die slow."

Mother dropped a knee on Jezebel's chest and wrapped her bony hands around her throat. Blood spewed from her slit lips and splattered all over Jezebel's face.

Her vision blurred and filled with black spots. A pressure built behind her eyes and she gasped for air. Jezebel ripped and pulled at

Mother's hands, but they held firm. The energy she used trying to escape only increased the pressure in her head. In a final effort, Jezebel reached up and jammed her thumb into Mother's eye, digging her nail deep into the socket.

Mother's grip loosened and Jezebel bucked her hips, sending her spilling over top. The sound of Mother's body skidding down the stairs was almost musical. She lay at the bottom, her right arm bent at an awkward angle and a sharp piece of bone protruding through the skin.

Jezebel took the stairs slowly, only stopping to grab the hammer from the toolbox. She loomed over Mother, disgusted by her mangled appearance.

"I used to wonder why I was made to endure this life," Jezebel said. "Then it came to me. I was put here to kill you."

The first blow of the hammer struck Mother's jaw, snapping the bone out of place. The second blow caved in her forehead, leaving a crescent shaped divot. After the third blow, Jezebel lost count. Crimson mist played through the air with every blow to Mother's head. Jezebel screamed and brought the hammer down again and again. Sections of Mother's skull split open and white lumps of brain matter squeezed through the cracks, reminding Jezebel of Samantha and how she used to push her stuffing back inside and sew her up.

Her hands cramped and her shoulders ached. Jezebel dropped the hammer and stepped away from the corpse. She leaned against the wall and let her body slide to the floor. She watched the blood leak from Mother's head and pool into a large puddle that seeped inside the gaps in the hardwood.

An hour passed before Jezebel shuffled to her bedroom, searching for sleep. She stripped off her clothes, annoyed by the dry blood stuck to her skin. Jezebel fell onto the bare mattress and snuggled into her thin blanket. The room was pitch black, the windows long since boarded over after her first escape attempt. She left the door wide open, embracing the freedom of sleeping alone in an unlocked room.

They would never touch her again.

PROTEIN

RACHEL NUSSBAUM

"FUCKING GROSS!" Anthony shouted from the kitchen. He always cussed, so David and Sandra didn't bother looking up from their respective tablet and phone.

"Fucking what is it?" Sandra called back, mocking his inflection.

"There's a nail in the pizza!"

"A what?" I asked.

"A. Nail," Anthony said, coming around the corner. "In our pizza."

"Like the metal kind?" David asked.

"Like the goddamn human kind that came off someone's nasty human finger," Anthony spat.

"Oh. Gross," David said, looking back down at his phone.

"There's sandwich junk in the fridge?" I offered.

"Just eat a piece without the nail on it," Sandra said.

"Dude," I said, crinkling my brows at her. "Ew."

"What? Too good for nail pizza?"

"Once a dish has human byproduct in it, the whole thing is contaminated," I explained.

"Siding with Tina, babe. Gross." David nodded.

"Nails aren't a byproduct," Sandra said. "They're adnexa. Skin appendages."

"Who gives a shit what they are?" Anthony barked. "David, gimme your phone."

"Gonna call the adhexa police?" David asked.

"*Adnexa* police," Sandra corrected.

"I'm gonna call the goddamn pizzeria who sold me this crap and tell them to refund me," Anthony replied.

"And by *me* you mean *us*, since all four of us went in on it, right?" David asked.

"Fuck off," Anthony said, bringing the phone to his ear and walking back into the kitchen.

"He's wound pretty tight."

"Yeah, he's having some money issues," I said. "Hours got cut."

Anthony's voice raised in the kitchen. David winced.

"Shit. I shoulda been nicer," he mumbled. "Is it 'cuz he complained about overtime?"

"Probably." I nodded.

" . . . Probably why he said we should skip the movie and just chill tonight," Sandra whispered.

"Dude," David sighed. "I'd have spotted him."

"Woulda made him feel worse," I said.

David turned a questioning glance to Sandra.

"Woulda," she agreed.

Suddenly, Anthony stormed back into the room, pizza box in hand.

"What did they say?"

"Asshole said he'd refund us, but we gotta bring the stupid pizza back," he barked.

"Seriously?" I said.

"*Company policy.* Because you know, fuck policy when it comes to not serving food with employee fallout, but how dare I expect to get my money back without proving it," Anthony spat, pulling out his keys.

"Want us to come with?" David said.

Anthony narrowed his eyes. "Why?"

Because you're hopping mad and dying to go off on someone and we need to keep you in check so you don't get your ass kicked, I thought.

"Eh. I'm pretty hungry. We could pick up some Chinese or a bucket of chicken on the way back," I said instead.

Anthony stood frozen for a moment, fists clenching and unclenching. Finally, he deflated. " . . . Yeah, okay."

Sandra shot me a thumbs up behind Anthony's back as we walked toward the door.

The smell of grease wafted through the car. I looked into the back seat—Sandra had cracked the pizza box and was peering inside.

"What are you doing?" I asked.

"I wanna see." She shrugged.

"Babe. Gross," David said, glaring up from his phone.

"I can't find it. Where is it?"

Anthony let out a sigh.

"Kind of close to the crust. Right by a pepperoni."

"Dude," David said, sinking down in his seat.

"I don't—oh. Whoa, weird," Sandra said. "It's a whole nail."

"What the hell did you think it was?" Anthony called back.

"A nail clipping, I guess. People don't typically lose their entire nail."

"It is kind of weird." Anthony said. "Fucked up hygiene practices aside, you'd think someone would feel it if their nail fell out."

"I lost my two big toenails once," I said. "When I went hiking with those shitty boots. They turned black and got loose and fell out like baby teeth a month later. I barely even felt it."

"Jesus christ, why are all of my friends gross?" David sighed into his palms.

"You love us," Sandra said, kissing his cheek.

"Keep your *fingernail-looking-at* face away from me."

As the two devolved into teasing, I faced forward in my seat. I noticed it then—the direction we were heading.

"Where are we going?" I asked. "West Beach isn't down this street."

" . . . I got it somewhere else this time. Found some coupon in the mail room," Anthony mumbled.

He looked embarrassed.

"That's fine, man," I said.

"I mean, it's not, it's pathetic," he said. "That I need a coupon to go in on a pizza three other people helped pay for."

"Dude. Everyone falls on hard times," Sandra chimed in from the back. "I almost had to move back in with my parents when I didn't get into the med schools I applied to."

Anthony sighed.

"I know, I'm sorry, I'm being a bitch. It just . . . it gets tiring, you know? Like no matter what I do, everything always goes wrong. Like now."

"Come on man. This is . . . just pizza, you know?" David said.

"Yeah man. Just pizza." I nodded.

Anthony was quiet for a moment before he forced a smile.

"Yeah," he said. "Just a stupid fucking pizza."

It was called Antonio's.

David leaned forward in his seat and grinned at Anthony as we pulled into the abandoned parking lot.

"Fucking what?" Anthony glared at him.

"*Ayeeee*," David said, snapping his fingers and pointing.

Anthony pushed him back by the face.

"Kay, back soon babe." David said, grabbing the pizza from Sandra.

Anthony and David got out of the car and hustled into the building. Up close, you could see just how run-down the place was. Several of the letters had fallen out of the rusty sign. Paint on the walls had peeled back in parts, revealing multiple coats over crumbled brick. The whole building seemed far too large for a hole-in-the-wall pizza joint. It had obviously been some other failing business at one point. Probably multiple points.

"This looks like the kinda place that would serve nail pizza on the reg," I noted as David and Anthony disappeared into the massive old brick parlor.

"Maybe not the reg," Sandra said. "Cooks only have so many fingers."

"Mmmm, yeah. Gotta choose what pizzas you wanna nail."

"Wanna hear my dark secret?" Sandra whispered.

I turned around and raised my brow.

"I still would have eaten it," she said.

"Yeah, you were hinting at it. It's still gross."

"Cooks have to touch pizza to make it—it's already touching their nails. Why do we draw a line? It's illogical."

"You're illogical," I said. "You're defending nail pizza."

" I'm really hungry and the pizza smelled good." Sandra sighed. "I just don't see the big deal. It's just protein."

Her phone pinged from inside her pocket. Sandra pulled it out and frowned.

"David says they need backup," she said, unbuckling her seatbelt. "Shit."

I hopped out of the car and followed Sandra to the door.

The inside of Antonio's was big and empty—poorly lit and as run down as it looked from outside. On the other side of the parlor, David and Anthony stood in front of the service counter. From the look on the poor cashier's face, she'd gotten an earful from Anthony already.

"I'm s-sorry sir, I didn't answer any phone calls."

"Bullshit, I just talked to some guy on the phone," Anthony said, slamming his fist down on the countertop.

"Dude." David winced.

He turned back to look at us and mouthed 'thank god' as we joined them behind the counter.

"What's going on?" I asked.

"This asshole—"

Sandra smacked Anthony, and he stopped talking.

" . . . Please don't swear, sir. We're a family establishment."

I glanced back behind the counter. The mousy cashier was tiny, probably still a high school student.

"No one else is here but us," Anthony mumbled under his breath.

Sandra smacked him again.

"Don't be rude." She turned to the cashier. "Is there a problem? We were told if we brought back our pizza we could get a refund."

"There's a fingernail in it," I explained.

The cashier opened and closed her mouth.

"I . . . there must have b-been a mistake," she said, voice shaking. "I'm the only employee here at the m-m-moment, and I didn't get any calls tonight?"

"That's bull—that's BS," Anthony said, glancing at Sandra. "I just called like twenty minutes ago."

"He did call." David nodded. "We were there."

The cashier blinked at us. With her big eyes and trembling lips, she looked like a deer in the headlights.

"I'm sorry, I didn't—"

"I . . . answered the call."

The saloon-style doors behind the young girl swung open, and a very, *very* large man slowly lumbered out of the kitchen.

"*Dad*," the cashier gasped, eyes practically bulging out of her head.

"Thought you were the only one here," Anthony mumbled smugly.

The cashier rushed over to the limping man. She held her hands out, like he was in danger of falling over.

As if her tiny frame could somehow support all four hundred pounds of him.

"Problem . . . with your pizza?" he asked, reaching the counter.

His voice was slow and labored and he took deep, gasping breaths. The name-tag pinned haphazardly to his apron read 'Tony'.

This was Antonio.

"We were the ones who just called," Sandra spoke up.

"Ahhh." Tony nodded. "So sorry . . . for your trouble. Did you . . . bring it with you?"

Every few words he spoke were punctuated by a wheeze. Tony slid the box forward. Tony's head swiveled down, and he stared at the pizza with unfocused eyes.

"I'll . . . make you a new one," he said, turning around.

"Whoa, wait! We want a refund, not a replacement!" Anthony sputtered.

"Gratuity," Tony wheezed, limping back into the kitchen. "Re . . . refund you too."

The saloon doors parted and he disappeared. The cashier glanced back and forth between us and the door.

"Shit," she mumbled, running after him, leaving us standing in silence.

"Yeah, so I'm never getting food from this part of town again," Anthony said, sitting down at a nearby table. "Lesson fucking learned."

"He didn't look so good."

I glanced over at Sandra. She'd been particularly quiet as we waited up till now.

"Tony?" I asked.

"Yeah," David agreed, abandoning the dust-coated pinball machine in the corner and walking over. "He seemed . . . not like, down's syndrome or anything just . . . kind of slow?"

Sandra shook her head.

"No, I mean he didn't look healthy. His skin was sallow and his eyes were all . . . " she trailed off.

"Like he was sick?" I asked.

"Like I'm not going to be eating any of that second pizza."

"What's taking him so long anyway?" Anthony huffed. "It's been half an hour."

"Well, you saw him. It probably takes him a while to do anything," Sandra mumbled.

"Well, now I'm actually really fucking hungry," Anthony said.

"Maybe we should just go," David suggested.

"He didn't give us our money back yet," Anthony said firmly.

"I know man, but ya know . . . this whole thing is really starting to skeeve me out. Maybe we should just grab some Chinese to-go."

"No way in hell, dude. I'm not letting us waste thirty bucks and all this time. We're at least getting our money back before we get out of here. I'll go ring the bell," Anthony sighed, getting up.

"Dude, don't," Sandra said. "You'll just interrupt him."

"Well, then I'm grabbing a soda from the fridge, I need some calories before I lose my goddamn mind."

Anthony trudged over to the clear-case freezer and grabbed a can of off-brand cola.

"Surprised this place is able to stay open. Think it's just him and his daughter?" I looked around the deserted pizzeria.

"This place seems one bad night away from going under. How were they able to afford printing and mailing out coupons?" David asked.

"I think the coupon was pretty old, to be honest," Anthony said sheepishly as he sat back down. "Someone'd left it behind in the mailroom under a stack of old catalogs."

He popped the cola tab and brought it to his lips. Seconds later, he spat soda across the table.

"Dude!" David shouted, yanking his hands back.

"Holy shit," Anthony gagged. "This is fucking nasty. It just tastes like chemicals."

Sandra raised an inquisitive eyebrow and took the can from Anthony, peeking underneath. "This expired last year."

"Of course it fucking did." Anthony slumped back in his seat.

"The hell is wrong with this place?" David straightened, looking back at the saloon doors to the kitchen.

"So many things. And now my mouth tastes like ass," Anthony mumbled.

"I left my green tea in the car," Sandra said, standing up. "I'll get it for you."

"Yeah. Thanks."

"Seriously, guys." David checked his phone. "I'll wait another ten minutes, and then I say we get the eff out of here."

"Seems fair." I nodded, glancing at at Anthony, waiting for him to protest.

The fire in his eyes had burnt down. Now he just looked plain defeated. He opened his mouth and closed it.

Across the parlor, Sandra shook the doorknob.

"Guys?" she called over. "It's locked?"

"What?" David asked.

Sandra rattled the door.

"It's . . . it's locked. The door's locked."

David and I stood up. He reached her first.

"Did it lock behind us?" David asked, trying the handle himself. "Oh, what the fuck?"

"I don't like this," I said, glancing around the brick parlor. I noticed the windows. How they were all far too small for anyone to fit through.

"Okay, fuck this," Anthony said, springing up. "Let's get out through the back."

Anthony took off down the back hallway that led to the bathrooms. David reached down and grabbed Sandra's hand, motioning for us to follow.

We didn't even turn the corner before we heard him scream.

I was the first to reach Anthony—who was down on his knees, vomiting. I put my hand on his back, and he spun around.

"Tina, holy shit. I was—she's . . . fucking hell . . . " he gasped, gagging.

I glanced behind me. The bathroom door was halfway open, and I could see something crumpled on the floor. I took a step forward and glanced in.

The cashier, lying in a pool of blood.

"What the fuck?!" David yelled from behind me, stumbling back.

I couldn't speak. Couldn't move. Couldn't even close my eyes and or look away.

Thick gashes littered her body. One split the muscle of her arm apart, another pair traveled across her middle, exposing a wedge of intestines. The wounds were pulpy, dark red and white. Meat and fat.

I leaned down next to Anthony and started vomiting too.

When the ringing finally faded away from my ears, I looked around in shock. Anthony was up and rattling the back door, while David and Sandra were perched over the cashier. I swallowed and picked myself up. Sandra turned around and held up a blood-splattered phone.

"She was trying to call 9-1-1," Sandra said.

"911, fuck, right!" David said, reaching into his pocket.

"Anthony?" I said, turning around.

"Fucking what?!" he yelled.

"You should be quieter," I whispered.

Anthony stared at me before realization dawned on him. He backed away from the doors.

"Yes, hello, please," David spoke into the phone. "Someone's been murdered and we think the killer is still in the building. Yes? Yeah, Antonio's, the pizzeria downtown . . . "

David's eyes widened.

"Wait, what?" he sputtered. "This isn't . . . but . . . "

He pulled the phone away from his face in shock.

"They . . . they said to stop crank calling them."

"What the fucking hell is going on?" Anthony whispered.

"I don't know," David said. "But we need to find a way out now."

He pulled himself to his feet, but Sandra stayed kneeling over the body.

"We gotta—"

"I don't think she's dead."

"What?" I looked over her shoulder.

Sandra reached up and yanked off her wool scarf.

"Try to stop the bleeding, hurry," she snapped.

"There's no way she's—"

"I can see her neck muscles clenching, she's alive!" Sandra said.

"Holy shit."

David crouched back down next to Sandra and helped tie the scarf along her butchered waist. I shook myself out of my stupor, hurrying to the sink.

"Paper towels? Water?" I asked.

"Paper towels. And a belt," Sandra instructed.

"I have a belt." Anthony's shaking hands went to his waist.

"Gimme!"

Sandra worked quickly, wrapping the roll of paper towels around the girl's arm and cinching them tight. She was good at this, calm and collected.

"It wasn't . . . his fault."

My heart slammed in my chest when the pained words rose up from the girl's bloody lips.

"He's not . . . he's not like this," she rasped. "He didn't mean to. I just . . . want him to go back . . . "

"That's good," Sandra said. "It's better if she can stay awake."

"Ask her how we can get out," Anthony said.

"Is it safe to move her?" I asked.

"I don't think we have much of a choice." Sandra nodded.

"Hey . . . " David said, meeting the girl's gaze. "Do you know how we can get out of here?"

"He . . . he took the keys . . . locking all the doors . . . " Her wheezing was as bad as Tony's.

Her head fell to the side, and a gash across her cheek split further. Drool, blood, and bits of gum dribbled out before Sandra plugged it close with a paper towel.

"Fucking hell," Anthony mumbled behind me.

Her face tensed as she swallowed.

"Event . . . event room."

David leaned down and Sandra helped pull the girl over onto his back. Once situated, we all hurried back down the hall, pushing open the doors labeled Event Room.

It was dark. We got a quick flash of the room—long plastic tables, stacked chairs, a small stage—before Anthony yanked the doors closed behind us and the room went pitch black. Sandra's hand wrapped around mine and together, we inched along the wall.

"Fuck . . . " Anthony whimpered.

Sandra pulled out her cellphone to illuminate our path. We worked our way to the back of the room, until we found cover behind the musty curtains of the stage.

We stood in tense silence—or Anthony and I did. Sandra got to work pulling out blue kiddy mats for the cashier, and David helped lay her down on them.

"My arm hurts . . . " she wheezed.

"I know sweetie, I'm sorry," Sandra hushed.

"Can we ask if she knows what's going on?" I whispered.

"I don't want to upset her."

"Her dad tried to fucking murder her," Anthony whispered. "I think that's as upsetting as it gets."

David and Sandra looked to each other. Sandra nodded, and David crouched down next to the girl.

"Hey . . . " David started. "Do you know . . . why he did this to you?"

"No," she wheezed. "But . . . I knew something was wrong. Something's been wrong for a long time."

The girl paused to take a deep breath.

"I tried to help. I wanted things to go back to normal. But he wouldn't tell me . . . "

"Can you tell us anything?" Sandra asked. "Anything you remember?"

The girl gasped hard. Sandra rubbed her shoulder gently.

"A . . . a man came. He looked . . . sorta sketch. Big tattoo on his neck. But . . . but he said he had a business deal for dad. Ever since, dad's been . . . different."

"Did you know what that guy wanted?" Sandra asked.

"I never saw him again," the girl whispered. "But . . . someone kept calling the police. They came a lot, but . . . they always said everything seemed fine. Just . . . some prankster. I really wanted to believe it, but . . . "

The girl sputtered, and blood bubbled up between her lips.

Sandra held up her hand to signal we were done with the conversation. I looked at David and Anthony.

"What the hell do we do?" I whispered.

"I don't know," Anthony said. "I don't fucking know—"

A large creak echoed from the other side of the room, and Anthony clamped his hands around his mouth.

A door slammed open, followed by a loud thud. Another. Footsteps.

David grabbed Sandra's hand. I held my breath. Too terrified to peek through the curtains and look.

And then the door creaked open. A moment later, it slammed shut and I breathed in relief.

"Holy shit," Sandra gasped.

"Where the hell did he come from?" David asked.

I slowly poked my head through the gap in the curtain, pulling out my phone and turning on the flashlight. It didn't provide much light, but I could make out a door on the other side of the room. I glanced at Sandra, holding the girl's hand tight, and David, gripping Sandra's shoulders.

Sandra wouldn't leave her, and David wouldn't leave Sandra.

"I'll go check it out," I whispered.

I slid out from behind the curtain and lowered my feet off the stage, shaking as I walked.

"Wait up!"

There was a shuffling behind me, and I turned to see Anthony following after. I nodded as he caught up to me and we continued together.

"I can't believe this is fucking happening, dude," he whispered.

"Me either."

"It's . . . is it really what it sounds like?" he asked.

"What's it sound like?"

"Sounds like the mob's been hiding bodies here. Like that fucker's been helping chop them up in his kitchen, and someone's fucking nail got in our pizza."

"Yeah." I nodded. "That's what it sounds like."

"Fucking hell," Anthony mumbled.

We reached the door and I eased it open. A staircase met us on the other end, descending into a basement. I took a few steps down, lighting up the dark room. Boxes, furniture, and another staircase on the other side of the room.

And then, my light landed on a window.

I turned around and blinked my light back at the curtain, signaling for David and Sandra to follow. Time passed painfully slow as they gathered the girl and caught up to us. I led the way as we descended the stairs, holding the light as Anthony and Sandra moved a table and climbed up to reach the window.

"Frick." Sandra tapped the window frame. "It's wired glass."

"The hell is that?" Anthony asked.

"It's got chicken wire embedded in it," Sandra said. "We'd have to pop the whole thing out of its tracks—"

"That's gonna be too loud."

I sighed and stared down at the floor. This was bad. This was all so bad.

And then I noticed the blood.

A small puddle by David's feet. I looked at the poor girl slung over his back. The scarf tied around her middle was sopping red. Her eyes were open, still and lifeless.

"David?" I whispered, my voice trembling.

He looked over at me.

"I think she's gone."

David stared back at me with wide eyes. Slowly, he lowered himself to the ground, easing the body off his back. Sandra jumped off the table and hurried to examine her. After a moment, she stood, bringing a hand to her mouth to muffle a sob.

"Didn't even know her name," David mumbled in shock.

We filed out of the basement quickly, eager to get away. David led us up the second staircase, peering out before signaling the coast was clear.

"The kitchen," he whispered as we followed him.

It was like a bomb went off. Flour and spills everywhere, forks and spoons littering the floor. On top of that, something smelled . . . bad.

Like spoiled meat.

"Knives, look for knives!" David said.

He and Sandra began tearing open drawers, looking for something to arm themselves with. Anthony didn't move. His eyes were blank and his mouth was trembling. I reached out to him.

"This is my fault," he whispered.

I opened my mouth to speak, but a horrifyingly familiar thud echoed from outside the kitchen.

"Fuck," Anthony said.

"Hide!" Sandra whispered.

I dropped low and glanced around the kitchen, looking for cover. There was only one place to hide, and we all scuttled to it as fast as we could.

The freezer.

Once all of us crawled in, David pulled the door shut.

I instantly brought my hands to my arms and shivered. "He's got us cornered."

"Not if he doesn't know we're in here," Sandra said. "So shut up."

"Keep looking, there might be something we can use in here!" David said, turning to the food storage shelves.

With no other options, I turned to the shelves with David. There were few prospects—moldy vegetables, stacks of cheese. I quietly began sifting through a crate of butcher wrapped meat.

"This is my fault," Anthony moaned again. "All of this is my fucking fault."

"Anthony, shut up and help," Sandra hissed.

"I got all of us fucking murdered over thirty dollars," he mumbled.

"Seriously, get a goddamn grip!" David spat.

It was painful shifting through the cold items, but I couldn't stop—every moment counted here, and we needed to find something we could defend ourselves with. I moved another piece of frozen meat and jerked back.

An eye. Peering through gaps of butcher paper.

I dropped the meat in my hand and scrambled away from the shelf, but the shift in balance sent the whole crate tumbling to the floor.

"Fuck!" David hissed.

A round, poorly-wrapped package rolled out, butcher paper unfurling as it did.

A frostbitten human head skidded to a stop at Anthony's feet.

I pulled my hands over my mouth, and David stumbled back, hissing out a string of curses. Anthony didn't do anything. Just stared down at the frozen face, trembling.

"We're gonna die here," he said.

From next to me, Sandra took a step forward. With a shaking hand, she pointed to the head.

"The neck," she said. "Look at its neck."

There wasn't much neck left to look at, but once I got past the pulpy stump, I saw it.

A splotchy tattoo of a spiderweb. A faded black widow cropped down the middle.

"That . . . that's the guy. The one the cashier mentioned."

"The mob guy?" Anthony whispered.

I nodded.

"Then why the fuck is Tony killing people?" he asked. "If he's not working for the mob, why is he doing this?"

I stared down at the head, like it could offer up answers. Not only was it severed, it was mangled. His jaw was pried open so wide it had to have broke before rigor mortis set in. I winced as I realized his cheeks were split all the way back to his ears.

From behind us, the door knob clicked open.

"Shit!!!" David yelled.

He threw his side into the door, slamming it shut. Sandra and I rushed forward to help him keep it closed, but even with the three of us, the door rattled in the frame beneath our weight.

David groaned as he dug his heels into the floor, his arm sliding against the metal with every thud. One particularly strong thud parted the door, and in the few seconds before we could slam it back, David's hand slipped between the gap.

The crack was only drowned out by David's shout of pain. He yanked back on reflex, and that's all it took. Sandra and I stumbled backward as Tony pushed his way into the freezer.

He wheezed hard in the doorway, splattered in blood, the cleaver clenched tight in his hand. I grabbed Sandra and yanked her back, but David had fallen to the ground. With a sputter, Tony lowered his gaze to him, and he slowly raised the cleaver over him.

"*Motherfucker!*"

The shout from the back of the freezer caught all of us—even Tony off guard. He froze, his head swiveling in confusion.

And in the next instant, Anthony came rushing forward past me, charging straight into Tony.

He had nothing. No weapon, no means of defense, nothing. But as strong and deadly as Tony had proven to be, Anthony seemed to remember what we all forgot about the last time we saw him.

He could barely hold himself upright.

Tony flailed his arms as he stumbled out of the freezer, and Anthony used the momentum to push him as hard as he could. The two of them toppled out of our line of sight, but I could hear them crash onto the kitchen floor. The sound was punctuated with startled cries from both of them, and what I could only describe as a *squish*.

After a long moment of silence, Sandra rushed forward to check on David. Cautiously—and with shaking legs—I walked out of the freezer.

Tony had landed on his back against the floor, and Anthony had landed on top of him. He seemed in shock, gasping hard above the unmoving behemoth. When he finally caught his bearings and rolled off of Tony, we could see it. The cleaver embedded in Tony's belly, and the blood bubbling out around it. Anthony had driven it right into him when they landed.

"Fucking shit," Anthony yelled, yanking himself off the floor and backing up into me. "Fucking, *fucking* shit!"

I looked down at Tony. His eyes stared blankly up at the ceiling lights.

"Is he . . . ?"

Behind me, David and Sandra crept up, and with a nod from David, Sandra lowered herself down to examine him.

"Careful . . . " Anthony warned.

Sandra stood still over his body for a few moments, while David joined her, unclipping the keys from Tony's belt.

"Something's not right here." Sandra furrowed her brows.

"What is it?" David asked.

Sandra gestured at him. Under the harsh kitchen light, I could make out details the dim lighting concealed back in the dining room. Tony's skin was . . . sickly. A pale, almost yellow hue. Stepping forward, I realized that terrible smell that permeated the kitchen seemed to be coming from him. I glanced down his arms, noting the veins and bruises.

His fingers.

He was missing several fingernails.

"He's . . . dead," Sandra said.

"No shit," Anthony mumbled.

"No," Sandra said, turning to look at us. "I mean, he's *been* dead. For a while it looks like."

Tony's body spasmed on the floor.

Sandra screamed. David grabbed her with his good hand and they leapt against the wall. Anthony scrambled back, yanking me alongside him.

From the ground, Tony twitched, fingers clenching and unclenching, legs kicking aimlessly. His lifeless eyes bulged and his neck swelled. His mouth snapped open, and I watched in horror as his jaw cracked and bent apart—the flesh of his cheeks splitting along with it, right down to his ears.

Just like the severed head in the freezer. Whatever happened to him was happening to Tony now.

With a few wet sputters, an oozing mass erupted out of Tony's mouth.

It was thick and slimy, and at the sight of it, I backed against the cupboards, unsure of what the hell was happening. David, Sandra, and Anthony looked equally horrified at the rising pale slime.

No.

Not slime. It was all connected, all solid—a neat, thick, uniform line, alive and wriggling.

It was a *worm*. A massive worm.

It rose up into the air, inch by inch. Twitching and twisting as it slithered further and further out. Anthony turned back to look at me, eyes blown wide in terror.

He opened his mouth to cuss, but nothing came out.

Slowly, the creature lowered itself next to Tony's body, coiling onto the floor. And the four of us, frozen in horror, could only watch as the thing slithered across the tiles and wriggled down the kitchen drain.

LOST GIRL, FOUND DOG

DANIEL J. VOLPE

BECCA HATED MEAN PEOPLE.
The man who put her into the trunk of his car after stuffing a dirty rag in her mouth was definitely mean. Worse than mean. The plastic ties the man used on her hands had cut the skin, and now they were numb. It was like she'd made snowballs with her bare hands and couldn't warm them up.

It was dark in the trunk as it bounced up and down, little bits of light peeking through. Her body rattled against the hard trunk surface, like they were riding on a trail. Becca liked riding her bike on trails, almost as much as she liked riding the Coaster. That was where she met the man, whom she *thought* was nice.

She had woken to a beautiful October day. The leaves were just starting to fall, and it was warm but chilly in the shade—perfect bike-riding weather. Not only were there a bunch of cool trails behind her house, a long time ago, the town planned to build train tracks but never finished. They made big hills of dirt, and when the construction was cancelled, the dirt remained, leaving behind a natural half-pipe. The *Coasters* as the kids called it.

Becca got there before anyone else and was in childhood bliss, rocketing up and down the Coasters. Her spokes clicked and clacked as she popped up on the other dirt side, taking a quick spin through a favorite trail of hers before shooting down the other side. In her mind, she was a pilot fighting aliens.

"Wow, that's pretty cool," a man's voice called out.

Becca slammed her brakes at the top of the hill and looked around. She squinted through the slits of sunlight filtering between the branches and leaves. Her eyes picked him up standing on the other side of the Coasters.

The figure waved and smiled.

Even from far away, Becca liked his smile. It was big, white, and shiny. His blond hair was brushed to one side and looked clean. He had no facial hair and deep green eyes. They sparkled nice, just like his smile.

"Are you coming back this way?" he asked. "I want to see it again."

Becca knew she shouldn't. He was a stranger. Though he looked like a nice stranger, not a mean one.

She nodded, her helmet wiggling just a little. She pushed it back into position, gripped her handlebars, and pushed off.

Becca wanted to yell 'wee' as she catapulted down the hill but didn't want him to think she was a baby. The beads clicked and wind rushed by as she defied gravity, going up the other side of the hill. She came to a stop a few feet from him. He was even nicer looking up closer.

"Wow, bravo!!" He clapped and took a step closer.

Becca smiled at him, pushing back a lock of hair that was peeking from under her helmet.

"Thanks. I've been riding the Coasters for years," she told him.

"Oh, jeez, where are my manners?" He stepped closer, almost to the front tire of her bike and held out his hand. "I'm Jasper."

Becca's father taught her to shake hands. He always told her never to shake hands sitting down. She didn't know if a bike counted, but she wanted to be on the safe side. Gently, she laid her bike on the packed earth and reached out to him.

"Becca," she said, taking his sweaty hand.

The change was instant and terrifying. His bright, pretty teeth flashed into a sinister grin. Those green eyes turned putrid and uninviting. Jasper's hand crushed hers in a bone-grinding grip, pulling her into him. He wrapped one arm around her neck and squeezed.

Becca didn't even get to scream as her world went dark.

Jasper Jenkins's body shook with anticipation. It'd been so long since he had a clean young girl. He'd worked a road crew over the last few years and been able to satisfy his bloodlust by murdering vagrants and prostitutes. If he had time and a good spot, torture. It was worth it just to feel their blood and warmth. But he never satiated his greatest desires with them. Consuming human flesh.

Now he had time and a perfect location. And sweet little Becca was going to be such a pure treat. Tender. His stomach growled with hunger.

He drove slow to protect his prize, but there wasn't much he could do to reduce the bumps on the rural roads of Elkpark in upstate New York. He'd searched all along the outskirts of Ashmore, the tiny village nestled between the Neversink and Delaware river searching for a spot. That's when he found the old hunter's cabin.

The car stopped in a cloud of dirt in front of the cabin.

The cabin was perfect for him. It only had two small rooms and a shallow root cellar with four steps leading down into it. There was no heat, though there was a wood stove, and no electricity or water. It was perfect. Jasper knew having utilities was a luxury but also produced a bill, which then created a record. That was something he didn't want.

Jasper opened the trunk and looked lovingly at the little girl, Becca.

She was sweating and started breathing harder at the sight of him.

He smiled, picking her up like a father about to put her to bed.

She thrashed weakly but stopped when he pinched her arm. She screamed through the gag.

"Now, that isn't how good girls act," he said, face to face with her. A welt was already rising on her arm. "If you're a bad girl, I'll hurt you." He smiled. "Understand?"

Becca nodded.

"Good girl," he said, carrying her into the cabin. The trap door to the cellar stood open and unceremoniously he dropped her into the dark hole.

Fall in the Northeast is a beautiful time, but it's also deadly. The sun and temperature plummet fast, often catching people unaware. It could be 75 degrees in the sunshine and within minutes drop down to 50 and below.

Jasper loved it. He watched twilight descend from the safety of his hideout. A gust of wind whipped against the slats of the cabin.

Jasper sat on an old chair, his feet up on a small table. A gas lantern was on the end table next to him, along with a glass of water. He had an old paperback in his hand, trying to read by lantern light. It wasn't easy, but it was better than nothing. He closed the book and opened the woodstove, stirring the embers and getting a rise of flame.

It wasn't that cold in the cabin, but the fire gave him something else to do besides read and think about Becca.

He wanted to start in on her; he had a new knife but decided to wait. Jasper didn't mind working in the dark but seeing their pain and fear was all part of the process. He didn't think the lantern would give him adequate light for his viewing pleasure. So, he used every ounce of his willpower and waited.

The fire was stoked and raging.

There was a knock at the door.

Jasper turned his head, eyes snapping, pulse racing. At first, he thought he was hearing things or maybe the wind had blown something against the cabin. The knock came again, more forceful this time.

Jasper stood, grabbing the fireplace poker and walking toward the door. His mind was racing on who would be out this time of night, in the middle of nowhere. It couldn't be the police, they wouldn't knock. His door would've been rammed in, and he'd been blinded by flashbangs. Honestly, if they knew what he'd done, what he was, they'd kill him.

"Hello," came a woman's voice. It wavered. "Hello, please let me in." Silence. "I saw you in the chair. Please, I'm hurt and lost."

Jasper relaxed but not completely.

Fuck, he thought. *If she saw me, then she knows I'm here. If I ignore her, she'll wander away, but if she finds help, they might come back here. If I let her in, people might be looking for her and come here.*

Another idea struck him, one of pure genius.

Or I let her in, kill her and the girl, torch the place and run away. When anyone finds the place, they'll think she was the killer.

It could work.

Jasper flashed a grin and opened the door.

She could have walked right out of his dreams. His eyes took her in, from head to toe in an instant, but he savored every detail.

The woman was tall, but not abnormally tall, about 5'9" if he had to guess. Her dark hair was wet and wrapped up in a messy bun, accenting her slender, pale neck. She wore a thin, button-up, long-sleeved shirt, which was open, revealing a wet, white tank top. Her bra, which was also white, showed through the wet shirt. Her jeans clung to her, also soaking wet.

She shivered in the doorway before walking past Jasper.

"Oh, God, thank you," she said, kneeling down in front of the woodstove. She put her hands in front of it, nearly touching the black metal.

Jasper had the poker in his hands as he walked toward her. "Here, let me help you," he said, using the metal hook to open the door of the stove.

A roiling inferno peeked out the black maw, flames licking at the dying log. He grabbed two fresh ones and slid them in, rekindling the weakening light.

"Oh, that's nice," she said, rubbing herself. "I'm sorry," she stood, facing him. "I'm Talia." She held out her now warm hand.

Jasper took it. He could smell her. A sweetness poured from her like the finest perfume mixed with scents you would find in a candy shop. It was heavenly. He felt himself start to swell. *Maybe I'll rape her corpse after I kill her,* he thought, shaking her hand.

"Jasper," he said, looking at her wet clothes. "What the hell happened to you?"

Talia laughed and shivered. "Well, I was out for a nice hike with a few friends, but they aren't nearly in as good shape as I am. So, in my stupidity, I hiked ahead and got myself good and lost. To make matters worse, I fell into the river, destroying my cell phone. It wasn't bad, but then the sun went down." She hugged herself for warmth.

A part of Jasper, an old part, wanted to help her. To give her a blanket or towel...to help her out of her clothes.

She looked into his eyes and smiled. The firelight of the lantern must've hit just right, because, for a second, Jasper thought her eyes turned red.

"Thank God I found you." She shivered. "I'm sorry to impose, but do you have anything dry I could wear? These wet clothes are killing me."

Jasper was almost in a trance. Her voice was oil on silk, the smoothness caressing his ears. A bead of water ran from her hair, sliding down her neck.

"Ah, yeah," he said.

She followed him into the small bedroom, the only other room in the cabin.

"Here," he said, handing her a t-shirt and sweatpants, hoping they were clean.

"Thank you." She put her hand on his chest.

His heart raced.

Jasper stepped out, giving her some privacy. He thought about little Becca in the cellar. He hoped her gag was tight.

Becca stopped crying. When the mean man (she wouldn't even think his name) threw her in the hole, it hurt. She didn't think anything was broken and that was good. She didn't want a cast for Halloween. It would be too hard to hold her candy.

The hole was small and dark, much darker than the trunk. She could hear the man walking around, but then she heard something else, a knock at the door.

Becca screamed and yelled, but her gag was too tight. It made her choke and cough. Her mouth was so dry, she would've done anything for a drink of water.

The hole smelled like a swamp. It was the same smell as when Becca stepped in black, swamp mud, that rotting stink she hated. After a while, she'd gotten used to it, but there was something new. A new smell.

It smelled like a dog, but not bad, like a wet dog, but just...dog. She thought she would panic if she were locked away with an animal, especially being tied up and gagged, but she didn't. The smell actually calmed her.

Her mind went back to Halloween and all the candy she was going to get.

Talia walked out of the room moments later. Her hair was towel-dried and down, laying damp across her shoulders and upper back.

Jasper could see she had taken her bra off as well. Her stiff nipples poked against the fabric of the t-shirt. Two lovely little tents. He couldn't place her ethnicity but had a feeling her areolas would be slightly dark. Not brown, but just a deeper shade of pink.

She caught him staring and smiled at him. "I'm just going to set my clothes on the chair to dry." She walked over and grabbed a chair, pulling it toward the woodstove. She draped her clothes over the back of it. Steam rose from them.

Jasper watched her firm ass shake in the sweatpants. She'd taken her underwear off, too. He felt himself growing hard. He knew he was a good-looking guy but didn't know if she'd fall for his advances. She also looked like she was in shape and would put up a fight if he tried to just rape her. His mind was made up, he'd try and see if he could seduce her first. If not, he'd go with plan b.

Talia turned and walked over to Jasper. Her lips seemed fuller, and her eyes darker.

"Thank you so much," she breathed, inches away from him. Her breath was sweet as if she were chewing tea-tree gum. Talia put a hand on his chest, feeling his racing heart. "I wish there was a way to repay you for your kindness."

Jasper was fully erect now, his jeans twisting his hard-on. This was one of the most insane things to ever happen to him, and he'd been a part of some crazy shit. It was like the stories in those seedy porno mags he read as a kid, not real life. A smoking hot woman didn't walk out of the woods, in the middle of nowhere, and fuck. It just didn't happen.

Her hand went to his crotch.

Well, he guessed it was happening now.

"Oh, I think *he* knows how I can repay you," she said, rubbing the head of his cock through his pants. She licked his lips, tasting him.

He couldn't take it anymore and kissed her. His ferocity was met by hers, their teeth hitting but neither caring.

She drove him back, pushing him into the bedroom and onto the bed.

The full moon peeked through the window, a voyeur taking a look. Jasper was thankful for it; he wanted to see this sexual goddess in all her glory.

Talia pulled her shirt over her head, revealing two heavy breasts. They had the perfect amount of natural hang. Her nipples were puckered from the cold and stood straight out, calling to Jasper. She fell to her knees in front of him, her hands rubbing his inner thighs.

"Take these off. Now," she demanded, stroking his painfully hard cock.

Jasper's fingers never moved so fast as he undid his jeans and yanked them off. His dick, slick with pre-cum, popped out as he kicked his pants away.

As soon as he crossed the room, Talia descended on him. She took him in her mouth, taking his length to the back of her throat.

Jasper watched her head bob up and down, her breasts swinging with each movement of it. He ran his fingers through her damp hair, grabbing a handful.

She moaned as he pulled it but didn't break her stride.

Jasper needed to stop her or he was going to blow his load. He needed her cunt. He didn't know why, but it was almost an animalistic need. There was something about her smell; it was driving him wild.

"Give me that fucking pussy," he said, pulling her hair hard.

Talia looked up at him, her mouth slick with spit and his cock juice. She smiled and stood up.

Jasper removed his shirt , showing off his chiseled muscles.

She looked lovingly at his hard body. "Oh, baby, you have no idea what you're in for." She let the sweatpants drop around her ankles, revealing her sex.

Jasper never thought vaginas to be overly attractive. Many were okay, but it wasn't something he looked at. A lot were razor-burned or too lippy, but not hers. It was perhaps the pussy of his dreams.

Talia was nearly clean-shaven. No, she had to be waxed. Her lips were bald with not a trace of stubble. Only the slightest, most delicate strip of black pubic hair was left. She stepped forward, her sex opening slightly, a bead of moisture running down the cleft.

Jasper nearly lost his load right there but held his composure. He lay back, watching her advance, shuddering as she straddled him.

Heat came off her vagina as she lowered herself, just touching the sticky tip of his cock.

"You want it?" she asked, staring at him. Her hands reached up and kneaded her breasts.

"You have no fucking idea," he moaned, willing her to descend and take him into her.

Slowly and with expertise, she lowered herself onto him. She shuddered, taking his whole dick to the base.

Jasper let out a sigh. Her tightness was nearly overwhelming. He'd had his share of pussy, but this felt like nothing he'd ever experienced. It was otherworldly.

Talia began to ride him. Her rhythm was perfect. Sometimes slow grinding to give her swollen clit some attention, then, when her feral lust grew too much, she'd be bouncing, slamming the head of his dick deep inside her.

Jasper lay on his back, with his eyes closed. He needed to will his orgasm away or he'd lose it and shoot his wad. He reached up, his hand touching a soft yet firm breast. He teased her nipple, rubbing between forefinger and thumb.

"Mmmm," Talia moaned, her hand covering his, rubbing her own breast. She put her free hand on his chest. "Do you like that?"

Jasper could feel his orgasm creeping in. He was almost at the point of no return. A few more thrusts from her sopping wet sex and that would be it.

"Fuck yeah," he breathed, opening his eyes to watch. He was buried deep inside her. He could feel her wetness running down his balls and he loved it.

"You've been a bad boy, Jasper Jenkins," she said, staring at him.

"Baby," he said, watching her ride him, "you have no idea." He paused for a second. *How the fuck did she know my last name?*

"You need to be punished." She rode him at a feverish pace, bucking up and down.

That was it, Jasper had reached the point of no return. It was the last and most painful orgasm he'd ever have.

Talia's pussy clamped on his cock, holding him in place. She changed in an instant. The fear on Jasper's face was enough for her to cum. Her body quaked as she transformed, waves of pleasure feeding on his horror.

Her hand on his chest was no longer thin and delicate but grotesque and tipped with dagger-like claws. She ripped through muscle and bone, slicing clean through his ribs. Talia avoided the heart; she wanted him alive just a little longer.

Jasper screamed, blood flowing from his chest. His hand, the one on her breast, now grasped coarse, black fur. He tried to pull it away, but it was caught in her vise-like grip.

Talia broke his wrist backward. Tendons and shattered bone poked from his skin.

He wailed just as his orgasm reached its crescendo. He couldn't help it, his body just reacted. The pleasure and immense pain was hot and cold, sweet yet bitter. A fierce blast of cum pumped into the beast on top of him.

Talia's face morphed, too. Her smooth skin was ridged, new bones growing underneath the old. Her mouth elongated and was now impossibly wide. She took his broken arm and bit down, severing it above the elbow. A gout of hot blood shot onto the wall, the brachial artery ripped to shreds. Talia's mouth was slick with gore. She smiled. Now, with both hands and her mouth free, she attacked in earnest. Razor sharp claws ripped the rest of his chest open. She spread his ribs, exposing the still-beating heart.

The organ fluttered; it was in panic mode as it tried to pump blood to the dying body. Its efforts were in vain.

Talia ripped it free, devouring it in one bloody bite.

Finally, the light went out of Jasper's eyes.

Talia was far from done. She opened his gut. The stench of stomach matter and shit filled the air. To her it was like perfume. Talia fed ravenously.

Becca woke up. She didn't mean to fall asleep, but she was so tired. In the moments before she was fully awake, she thought her room smelled funny. Her eyes fluttered open, and she panicked. She wasn't in her room at all. The hole. She was in a dirt hole. And the meanie weenie. He threw her in there. She put her hands to her mouth to stifle a cry.

My hands, she thought, *they're free.* She looked at her wrists, which were cut from the plastic ties, but unscathed. Her feet were also free and she was ungagged.

A bar of morning light shone through the trap door where the man had thrown her. The door was open now, revealing a steep ladder.

Something walked into the light, and Becca shrieked. She caught herself, not wanting to let the man know she was awake.

It was a dog. The dog sat in the light, its tail wagging. Her black fur looked like oil in the light.

Becca put a hand toward the dog, hoping she wouldn't bite.

The dog let out a happy yip and walked over to sniff her hand. The cold nose felt nice. Then he licked her fingers, tail wagging the whole time.

"Shhh," Becca told the dog. "There's a mean man upstairs." For some reason, she didn't think that was true any longer though. Something felt different.

The dog walked away, mounting the ladder. With a step and a hop, the dog went up, looking down at Becca.

Becca stood on wobbly legs and climbed out. The only other door in the cabin was shut, and this made her happy. A very bad smell was coming out of there. She pet the dog, who looked up at her.

"Come on, let's get the hell out of here," Becca said. She thought her mommy and daddy would forgive the bad word.

Becca never had a pet before. Daddy was allergic to cats and mommy hated dogs. She thought her mommy might make an exception for this one.

The pair walked away from the cabin, a girl and her dog, toward the sounds of traffic.

ABOUT THE AUTHORS

Born in Halifax, Nova Scotia, Canada but now living in Tianjin, China, **Ryan Dyer** has been covering the morbid and sensational tales of the orient for the past decade. When he is not watching horror films, writing about Asian bands or trying odd cuisines, he is often relaxing at home with his wife Betty and his cat Ash.

Arlo Gorevin's work has appeared in *Hellhound Magazine*, the *Cosmos Hundred Word Horror Anthology* from Ghost Orchid Press and the *666 Dark Drabbles Anthology* from Black Hare Press. He hails from Manchester in England and is a slave to two potentially demonic cats.

Zoltán Komor lives in Hungary. He writes surreal short stories and which have been published in several literary magazines (*Caliban Online, Drabblecast, The Phantom Drift, Gone Lawn, Bizarro Central*, etc.). His first English book, titled *Flamingos in the Ashtray: 25 Bizarro Short Stories*, was released by Burning Bulb Press.

Lucy Leitner is an advertising writer and award-winning journalist in Pittsburgh, PA. Her transgressive fiction includes the novels *Outrage: Level 10* and *Working Stiffs* as well as several shorter works that appear in anthologies and godless.com original series. She co-hosts the *Horror Business* podcast with S.C. Mendes.

W.R. Macumber was born in a small town and learned to live in a small town, then moved to a small city. He writes from a rickety wooden desk somewhere in the wilds of central Canada. He has a love affair with the macabre and writes fiction in the spaces between family life and training/competing in Mixed Martial Arts. W.R. is currently working on multiple writing project

S.C. Mendes is the co-host of Horror Business—a podcast dedicated to helping authors make a career of their writing. He is also the co-owner of Blood Bound Books—an independent publisher whose mission is to spreading hope through dark fiction.

Lucas Milliron's fiction spans a broad spectrum of horror. His stories range from cosmic to kinky horror, varying from mildly spooky to extreme acts of human depravity.
Find more at lucasmilliron.com

Nikki Noir writes erotic thrillers, extreme horror, and bizarre plotlines. Her fiction can be found on Godless and Blood Bound Books. Her visual art and love of all things spooky can be found at That Spooky Beach on IG and TikTok.

Rachel Nussbaum is a writer and artist from the Big Island of Hawaii. Her short stories have been featured in multiple anthologies, including *Brewtality* from The Evil Cookie Publishing and Blood Bound Books own *Night Terrors III* and *Crash Code*. Rachel recently had her first novella, *We Rotted in the Bitterlands*, published from Mannison Press. She hopes to keep writing (and one day illustrate) her own short stories, novels, and comics. Follow her on Goodreads at https://www.goodreads.com/author/show/7980391.Rachel_Nussbaum and Instagram at RachelNussbaumwrites

Daniel J. Volpe is an author of extreme horror and splatterpunk. His love for horror started at a young age when his grandfather unwittingly rented him *A Nightmare on Elm Street*. Daniel has published some of his stories with Raven's Inn Press, Sirens Call publications, Twisted Tales, Exiles Literary magazine, Literati Publications and self publishing. His novella, *Billy Silver* has received praise from many readers and authors alike, including Edward Lee and Dustin LaValley. He can be found on Facebook @ Daniel J. Volpe, Instagram @dj_volpe_author, Online at https://danielvolpe909.wixsite.com/danieljvolpehorror and Shitfist.com

Thomas K.S. Wake was tempered by the shamanic winds, a thousand lakes with a thousand stories, the whispers of the birch filled forests of gloom. He fell in love with horror at the tender age of 6 when he saw *Re-Animator* on VHS. That led him to search for the source story and that was it.

Consuming book after book, a thought popped into his head. One of being a writer and conjuring up something that would intrigue the minds of readers like his mind was intrigued. Living in Finland presented an obstacle though; there wasn't a horror culture to speak of there. Very few novels and even fewer horror films were made in the Land of Northern Lights. Horror was and still is, considered less, something not worthy of the creative efforts. This forced Thomas to seek publication abroad, and finally slowly, but steadily his stories are gaining traction. Now with almost after a year of hiatus, he is back at the keyboard, ready to horrify and terrorize readers.

Find more at www.thomas-wake.com

Matthew Weber is author of the books *Teeth Marks, A Dark & Winding Road, Seven Feet Under* and *The Bull*, and he is editor of the *Double Barrel Horror* anthology series. He also wrote and illustrated the children's book, *I Want to Be a Monster When I Grow Up*. He has served as editor-in-chief of *Extreme How-To* magazine since 2003 and is also author of the non-fiction book, *The Quick & Easy Home DIY Manual* (Weldon Owen Publishing). He lives just north of Birmingham, Alabama, with his wife, two sons and a daughter. When he isn't chasing kids, writing or remodeling, he plays bass guitar for the punk band SKEPTIC? Find him online at www.pintbottlepress.com.

Montague White, otherwise known as The Professor, emerged from the shadows to claim first prize in the 2021 KillerCon Gross Out Contest. He is now a regular presence on Godless, presenting deranged twists of classic works of horror literature every month.

Jay Wilburn is an author of horror and speculative fiction that lives in coastal South Carolina near Myrtle Beach. He is doing very well following a life-saving kidney transplant. He taught public school for sixteen years before becoming a full-time writer. His signature series is the *Dead Song Legend* Dodecology and for younger readers, *The Lake Scatter Wood Tales*. Follow his many musings @AmongTheZombies on Twitter, the Jay Wilburn author page on Facebook, and at JayWilburn.com. Jay Wilburn has a lot of original content on his Patreon page including a serial vampire novel and more. Patreon.com/JayWilburn Or catch him streaming live on Twitch. Twitch.tv/JayWilburn

Patrick Winters is a graduate of Illinois College in Jacksonville, IL, where he earned a degree in English Literature and Creative Writing. His work has been featured throughout several magazines and anthologies. Winters is an avid listener of all things hard-rock and heavy-metal, a compendium of comic-book knowledge, can (and will) do a perplexing array of voice impersonations, and can bend his thumbs further back than any person should have the right/capability of doing. It is all quite odd . . . A full list of his previous publications may be found at his author's site: http://wintersauthor.azurewebsites.net/Publications/List

www.ingramcontent.com/pod-product-compliance
Lightning Source LLC
Chambersburg PA
CBHW021922170626
46807CB00007B/2937